THE COLD CONSPIRACY
By Ed Dice

Chapter 1

Danny always liked the sound of a train, off in the distance, rumbling through the cold night air. Not being able to fall asleep before midnight he often heard it around that time. With his window cracked and on a clear night it sounded like it was only a few hundred yards away. For some reason it gave him solace knowing it was there, right on schedule. He imagined the people working on it, riding the rails 24-7 in a world that never slept. It was comforting to know that railroads were still in use in our modern world. With all our high tech gadgets and innovations we still needed big old steel wheels driven by high pressure fossil fuels running along metal rails set on wood. Railroads were first used to open up the west several hundred years ago and they really hadn't changed all that much since then. One of the first books Danny read in grade school was on the building of the transcontinental railroad. He could picture the Chinese workers employed to do most of the grunt work and wondered how many died in the process. Times were indeed tough back then. No one had trouble sleeping at night, people were kept busy just surviving and could ill to afford lie awake worrying about their problems.

Without electricity, most went to bed when the sun went down and awoke when it came up.

Danny thought how odd it was what with lights and TV and radio and such that we evolved into a society whose biggest defect is perhaps that we simply don't get enough sleep anymore.

Then it occurred to him that besides not enough sleep, surely we have too much of everything, too many choices. And then Danny's mind would wander and he would think about things that possibly no one else ever did.

Too many products, too many things to do, too many things to worry about, too much food, too much technology, too much of just about everything. Do we really need two thousand TV channels? Must we take pictures with our phones or watch music videos on them? How many kinds of chain restaurants can we over eat at? At what point will our internal "C" drive crash causing us to seek out too many doctors who will prescribe way too many pills? Is it possible the natives living in grass huts in Fiji know something we don't and is that why they all live to be 102?

The sound of the train peaked as it neared the old bridge about a mile from Danny's house and he purposely erased all his combobulated thoughts and concentrated solely on it. He waited for the whistle now, blowing once then shortly after a few quick bursts as it neared the crossing. After that, the rattle of the wheels and the sounds made by the large engine slowly trailed off into the distance. He closed his eyes and entered the world of darkness, where the tiny bits and pieces of all the data stored in his gray matter would evolve into surreal scenes of his utmost passions, desires and fears.

The blaring of the phone caused Danny's heart to jump. It was after 1 AM and although he was used to occasional late phone calls he hated them none the less. He hoped the phone wouldn't wake his wife, but let it ring one more time knowing his phone machine would pick it up, which it did. But now he was awake and there wasn't another train coming along to lull him back to sleep either. Damn, he thought, may as well use the bathroom since I am up. As he made his way back from the john he wondered why phones had to have such an alarming sound. Couldn't someone invent a phone that gently informed you of an incoming call? I mean seriously, with all our technology why not tell you who is calling. "Mr. Edwards, it seems you have an incoming message from the Davis residence. They are still waiting for you to pick up. Last chance. OK I will store the number for you to return the call at a more convenient time if you wish. Thank you."

But no, we still have this antiquated method of scaring the bejesus out of each other with this crude blaring of loud bells.

Maybe Danny would invent something like that and get rich from it. He could picture himself on the cover of Forbes magazine, maybe even on Letterman, clowning around with the king of late night. More crazy ideas filled his mind as he laid back down and tried to return to an unconscious state where nobody could bother him, and if they did he would at least wake up from it. But once more the blaring of bells in the darkness aroused him. He reached for the phone this time. He had older kids living away from home and 2 calls in a row could be important. "Hello" he said in a voice that had just been startled out of a deep sleep. There was a pause on the other end and then a response, "Sorry Mr. Edwards, this is Jim Woods, the night shift operating engineer at the Valley View mall. I am new here and saw your number listed for the mechanical contractor who has the HVAC contract for our facility."

"Yeah, that's me," said Danny, trying not to sound dismayed at being woken up in the middle of the night. Danny was a small time contractor who carried some big accounts. He certainly didn't want any of his large commercial customers to think he had some rinky-dink operation.

He had used professional phone answering services in the past but dropped them after a time. I mean, with cell phones and voicemail who really needed them? All they did was call you right after they were called anyway. Although it did give a more professional appearance most customers knew when they were talking to an answering service and Danny knew his work ethic and good reputation was usually enough to keep him busy.

The conversation continued.

"I thought I could get you scheduled to come out first thing in the morning to have a look at one of our main air handlers. I think we have a bad bearing, it's noisy as hell. What with the holidays approaching, the last thing we can afford is to shut down a main unit. It started getting really bad a few hours ago."

Danny said he would be out first thing and take a look see.

Danny had some small jobs in the morning but they would have to wait. This type of customer always came first. It was top dollar and steady work. His theory was you had to keep these types of customers happy. In an instant they could pick up the phone and call someone else. Losing accounts like that could be devastating to a small contractor. He needed them and built his business on them.

All the other work he had was gravy compared to the "big boys" he took care of.

He maintained high levels of insurance just for them. His personal attention to them often was the determining factor in keeping their fingers from doing a little walking in the yellow pages.

Now if only he could drift off to sleep, but his mind kept wandering. He pictured himself walking into the mall before it opened. He would first go into the management office to get clearance and then strut around like he owned the place. Maybe he liked that part of the biz the most. Going into places most have not dared. Walking through those doors marked authorized personnel only. He always said with a tool belt and company shirt, along with the confidence that you actually belong there, you could most likely walk into any building and not be bothered. At least that had been his experience. As he began to doze off once again, he saw himself analyzing the problem. Yep, it was a bearing going south. The night shift engineer was right. They usually were too. It was cheaper for many big companies to contract out this type of work rather than maintain the necessary staff for such repairs. They hired qualified help but found it hard to pay top dollar for guys who worked on major repairs such as this. It was good for them and good for guys like Danny.

He was now fast asleep. He dreamed he was in an old hall that had been converted to office cubicles, but he was lost and the A/C units were in bad shape. A large chandelier hung from the ceiling. He couldn't find his way around and when he left to go his truck it was gone. An alarm went off in the building and he and another guy found an old van that hadn't been started in many years, it was loaded with newspapers. On the stack of papers on the front seat was one from 1968 that headline read,

"Bobby Kennedy had been shot." The truck started up but before he left he had to go back and tell the office manager that he needed to replace the entire HVAC system. He wanted to take some of the old papers for collector's items but when he returned to the old van, someone else already had.

Then he noticed for some strange reason he was in his underwear. What a weird dream, even for Danny who often felt his dreams predicted the future, not exactly or with any rhyme or reason, but with some regularity similar to the more common feeling of déjà vu. What occurred the next day and subsequent week was more like a nightmare, one Danny could only wish he would awake from..

Danny heard his wife going off to work. She was a school teacher and was always up bright and early. Her job enabled them to live very comfortably at this point in their lives. And it gave her a sense of self esteem that many women who don't work may not have. They had been through the tough years long ago. She had quit her job when their first child was born, to stay home and raise him. She wanted no part of daycare or sitters. The last thing she wanted was to come home from work and have some stranger tell her what milestone her child had accomplished that day.

Those years for the Edwards were tough indeed. Small children, one income from a fledgling business with very little work at times. Danny often wondered how they survived. But the time flew by, eventually she returned to work after the kids were in school, and here they were, in their late 40's seemingly on cruise control and better off than any other time in their lives. Danny's business had survived the tough years and was now established. With a decent customer base and substantial cash flow he had found his niche in the market. A small service oriented company, low overhead and catering to reputable clients who trusted him and his work. He had considered going big several times, especially early on. Hiring many employees, taking out various ads and building up the business into your typical large company. But perhaps it was Danny's compulsion for detail that prevented him from doing so. He just had to feel he was in control of every aspect of his life. He found it hard to not recheck the work of his helpers. And then there was the matter of the family business he had started out in.

Fresh out of college with a relatively generic degree, Danny had returned home with his bride and took up working for the family's mechanical contracting business. It was suppose to be a temporary job until he found one where he could put his college education to work. But Danny had always liked working with his hands and there were few things he couldn't fix. He spent much of his childhood working on and building stuff, usually by himself and often in the garage of his middle class home in the suburbs.

He continued to work in the family business and felt at home there. But in time he grew frustrated with it. As many family operations turn out, too many differences of opinion, too little money to go around, too much stress. The company had grown large and seemed to be spiraling out of control. In time, Danny left and the family business floundered and then died, filing bankruptcy. As hard as it was for Danny to start out on his own, it was the best thing he ever did, even through all the hard times, he never regretted it. In the end, it had worked out for him.

He had one full time employee and a list of part time guys he could count on to help out for the bigger jobs. He had no long term plan, he just took things as they came, tried his best and hung in there. I guess that was also Danny's plan for life.

Danny made his way downstairs and grabbed a cup of coffee, the timer was set so every morning it was ready for him. He couldn't imagine waking up in the morning without it. He probably drank too much of it but there were certainly worse addictions out there. He detested those fancy, flavored coffees or newfangled concoctions that Starbucks built it's fortune on. Danny would only drink a fresh, regular cup of Joe with a bit of cream in it, thats it.

It was 6:45 and he had to get his ass in gear if he was to get to the mall before they started getting bent out of shape over their malfunctioning system. He hit the shower, put on his work clothes, grabbed another cup of Joe and fired up his van. It was a cloudy, late autumn day, the smell of fall was in the air. Someone had a wood burner going and it added to the aroma of the upcoming winter that was on the horizon. He pulled out and headed for the parkway hoping the traffic was light. He was waiting for a call from the mall maintenance supervisor as he drove toward his destination. They would get anxious in times like this. It was their job on the line should a major problem arise at the mall that went unresolved.

Although it was autumn and the nights were cool, the days were still somewhat warm. Most commercial buildings and malls used their air conditioning late into the seasons. The buildings heated up fast from lights, people, machinery and the like. No, they would not need heat today, they would need to have a functioning air conditioning system and Danny knew that well.

The preseason holiday shopping had already begun. It seemed to start earlier and earlier every year. Soon as the Halloween decorations came down, Santa was ready to start promoting everything and anything. Danny knew the panic mode that would set in should any potential shoppers leave their credit cards in their wallets and go somewhere else to shop, somewhere where it wasn't so damn hot. He had been under the gun before many times and knew it was part of the business. He didn't mind pressure but disliked it on a daily basis.

However, this call would be more than just the usual panic mode emergency type. It would start Danny through a whirlwind trip, one he would just as soon avoid.

Chapter 2

Danny used his cell phone to call his only full time employee, Bill Strathmore, a young guy who went right into the Army after high school. He got out of the service and went to trade school for 2 years. He called Danny's office looking for work upon graduation and fortunately Danny had just acquired some new accounts that would take up a lot of his time. Bill started working the next day and never looked back. He had learned the text book stuff in school and now he was learning the "hands on" of the trade. A good, honest worker who was recently engaged to the mother of his four year old daughter, Bill could be trusted and relied on. Danny gave Bill the jobs he was planning on doing before the mall called him with the emergency work.

Danny and Bill basically worked out of their trucks and homes. Danny had a small office front and storage area with some file cabinets, a computer and bathroom but the truth is, they hardly ever used it other than for paperwork, tax returns and an occasional place for parts and equipment. It was a legitimate tax deduction and Danny felt it made his operation seem more professional as well. He also received some of his mail there.

Danny pulled into the mall parking area and drove further in next to a loading dock, near the mechanical room. He put a sign on his windshield that read "Emergency Service." He checked into the management office, got a visitors pass and headed down the hallway towards the maintenance office. He would check in with them and find out exactly where the problem was.

This was all very routine for Danny. Different customer, different system, different day, that's all. As he headed down the long hallway with electrical conduits above and an occasional disconnect switch here and there, he passed another contractor heading out of the building. Hmm, he wondered, judging by his hand tools, that guy looked another HVAC repairman. He had on typical work clothes and bleach blond hair. As he passed, Danny turned and saw a company logo and name on the back of the guys jacket, "Environmental Air Quality Inc. " But Danny's was the only service truck in the parking lot that early in the morning. Had someone else been called in? Did the night shift guy not relate to the day engineer that Danny was coming in first thing? If he had lost the job, maybe the last cup of coffee took a little too long. He ran into Fred Ward, the head maintenance engineer, coming out of the office. Fred was an easy going, heavyset older guy with thinning black hair. He wore dark rimmed glasses and dressed in khakis and a collared shirt. His days of actually working on things were past. He had done his time in the field, over 35 years, and was now content to ride out the rest of his years in a management position. Her had been with the mall for nearly 8 years now and counted the time till he could retire. Soon as he reached age 65 he was "outta there." He would take the social security, his savings, cash in some mutual funds and sell his nice big house and head south with his wife and golf clubs. He couldn't wait, he told practically everybody he met about his master plan.

"Hey Danny", Fred said, "Wondering if you got that message from the night shift guy, we were stating to get a little panicky here, it's heading into prime time for us ya know. Can't afford a shut down this time of year."

Danny fully expected that and asked, "Hey Freddie, who was that other contractor I saw leaving, just curious?" Hoping to hear it was most likely someone called in from one of the retail stores for a separate repair that didn't involve the mall account.

Fred said, " I don't know, I didn't see anyone back here. Anyway lets get you back to air handler #2 and take a listen to this baby, something's not sounding too good, we think it's the main bearing, I hope at least the shaft is OK. Tearing all that apart could take some time, and who knows if the parts will be readily available?"

"Lets not jump the gun Freddie, we'll cross that bridge when we come to it," replied Danny.

The main bearing was indeed shot, the metal on metal grinding was consistent with a bearing going south. Danny had heard them sound a lot worse so he assumed it was in the early stages of deterioration. At this point the shaft was probably OK and swapping out the bearing and aligning the pulleys wasn't too bad of a job. He took some numbers and called Bill, his cohort in crime. "Hey Bill, wrap up whatever you are doing and stop by the supply house and pick up one of these parts for me, I'm down here at the Valley View mall, here are the numbers." Danny gave him the part numbers and told him the best place to go for them, he would call first and put them on order. He told Bill which section of the mall he was in, a place familiar to Bill. He had helped Danny work on those units a few times in the past "I'll shut this down and start tearing out the old one. We can't have this unit down for very long you know. Let me know if you have any problems, OK? See ya."

Bill finished up the small repair he was on and headed down the highway to the supply house, an HVAC parts distributor that only sold wholesale to licensed contractors. In short order he was at the job site with the bearing. With two of them now working on the unit it was repaired in less than an hour. Before they started it up Danny decided to take a look at the other back bearing on the far side of the massive air handler. Danny figured the mall maintenance crew had already greased it on their PM schedule but he wanted to double check it. He was very particular and liked to make sure he had checked everything possible so they wouldn't be calling him back next week. That didn't look good in his opinion. Even if you repair something on a system and something else completely unrelated to it breaks soon after, the powers that be may think it is your fault. That's how people are, some are more understanding than others though. So he would check it none the less.

The return ductwork was somewhat in the way and as he made his way around it, he dropped his nut driver on the floor in a darkened area on the room. "Damn it" he said. "Hey Bill can you see where that went, it headed over to the back by the wall." Bill got down on his knees and said "I see it, back there by the drain line." Danny replied, "OK it is closer to me, I got it." After he retrieved the tool, he glanced over at the back of the return duct, where the recycled air from the mall was drawn into the air handler to be either heated or cooled depending on the need. The faded old sheet metal had an access panel missing. It was a small opening to take temperature readings or visually check the motorized fresh air dampers. The panel was lying on the floor behind the duct. Danny squeezed back there and picked up the panel to pop it back on. As he did he figured since he was there why not check the dampers as well. He somehow managed to squirm his tiny Maglight in there and take a peek. Looking down he saw something he had never seen inside ductwork before. A small, cardboard looking canister with tiny holes in it laying down on the bottom, inside the ductwork. It almost resembled a rodent bait trap.

Were rats getting inside the air conditioning system? Although little varmints were common vandals to many mechanical systems, eating wires and insulation and nesting where it is warm, it was rare to find them actually inside the systems. The constant movement of air was enough of a deterrent to make sure most of them resided somewhere else. Still, nothing wold surprise Danny anymore and he was about to reinstall the metal patch and get his head out of there as his twisted neck was crying out to do so. That's when he saw it. Danny removed his head, focused his light a little better and asked Bill for an old milk carton, which was lying on the other side of the mechanical room. Now standing on the make shift stool he got a good look down at the box. What the hell Danny thought. Is that an air freshener or an insect repellant or what? Danny said, "Hey Bill, look at this." They switched places and Bill took a gander. "I ain't been in this biz nearly as long as you Dan but that's news to me." Bill replied. Danny said, "Go find Freddie, I want him to see this."

Freddie was at a loss as well. Matter of fact, he had never noticed that access panel either, being it was in such a hidden location. Even if he had seen it, Fred probably would have ignored it anyway. But one thing Fred Ward knew for sure, no one had authorization to put anything into the air conditioning system like that without him knowing about it first. Fred dug a clothes hanger out one of the lockers. He stretched it out and bent a hook on the end. Since Bill was the thinnest one of the group, as old age had yet taken its toll on his midsection, he wriggled up on the milk carton and reached down inside the massive duct with the hanger. He hooked it on the first try but as he lifted it up, it burst into one huge puff of smoke and for all practical purposes, disintegrated. What was left was some plastic, burnt cardboard and tiny pieces of wire with the insulation now gone. It fell off the hanger and back down to bottom the duct. It smoldered some more and soon only ashes remained. At this point Fred decided to turn the air handler back on, the event was over and the supply temperatures on the computer screen were rising. Stores were just now opening up their bar gates and shoppers were already pouring in the mall. The frequency drive slowly built up speed and the awful grinding noise was gone.
Fred called security and asked them to view the log file for the day. The log was empty so far except for Danny, Bill and one other entry. Environmental Air Quality Inc. had registered early and listed one of the franchise stores as it's customers that needed service. The store marked was Lydia's, an exclusive ladies chain store that was in all the big malls nationwide. Although the mall provided the main air conditioning for them, the individual stores were responsible for any problems that their area had such as controls, vent adjustments and the like. A typical mall log had any number of vendors listed on any given week. Fred asked Danny, "so you saw some guy coming down the hallway here on your way in?" "Yeah" Danny replied, "for a minute I thought you called someone else." Even when individual stores called in separate contractors, they had no business being down by the main mechanical rooms, they were maintained by either mall

personnel or those with contracts to be there, such as Danny's company.

Fred said, "well then what the hell was that guy doing down this way? Even if he got lost the clothing store was on the 2nd level of the mall and completely at the other end. He surely wouldn't be roaming around way down here in the basement."

Fred, Danny and Bill, all now wondering about the box and the smoke and the mystery visitor, headed up to the ladies clothing store, perhaps they had some answers. As they hit the 2nd level of the mall Danny asked Fred, "Who is that Environmental Air Quality outfit anyway? One of those air quality experts springing up these days? Ya know the kind, they convince everyone that they are sick due to bad air and sell policies to clean it up. I mean, who hasn't had an occasional headache or sick stomach at work. How hard would it be to convince them it is due to poor air quality? Nice little operation huh Freddie," Danny chuckled. "Many employees are just looking for an excuse like that" Danny continued, ,"Why hell, people in general think all kinds of things are bad for them these days. Watch the news, first it is good for you and then it causes cancer, what are you suppose to believe? I think we are creating a society of hypo's myself," Danny now really getting into his mental evolutionary theories." Every other commercial or ad is for drugs these days. Ya know how much money is involved in that?"

They arrived at Lydia's, an exclusive clothing store. A tall brunette met them at the counter and recognized Fred. She said, "What's new Fred, how have you been, got a problem in here we don't know about?" Usually maintenance men didn't show up at the storefronts unless they were called in. Even then it could take some time for them to show up, what with all the regular duties they had to address on any given day.

Bill nudged Danny and rolled his eye. Danny smirked looking at the big busted store clerk in high heels, dressed to the hilt. The employees in most of these stores looked like models but with a few years on them. It was the image Lydia's wanted to create for its customers. By shopping here you will look like this. Danny

often wondered how much planning went into large scale
operation such as these franchise stores. Every small detail
matters. Things you may not consciously notice such as lighting,
displays, flooring, counter tops, mannequins and of course
employee appearance could be the difference in success or
failure. There was so much competition anymore. In stores like
this, price was not often much of a determining factor. People
who went there had money. Matter of fact, the more they paid for
it the better it usually made them feel. They were searching for a
certain look, something exclusive and obviously different from
the run of the mill individual you pass on the street. And that took
money, which most of their regular customers had plenty of.
Occasionally a younger girl would come in, often with her mom,
looking for a prom dress or something for a special occasion, and
they sold to quite a few to those types as well. But the majority of
their sales were to professional working women or wives and
daughters of men who wore a nice suit to work. Lawyers,
bankers and big shots with nice cars and big houses kept stores
like this in the black ink, or so it seemed.
"Who are your buddies Fred?" She asked. "This is Danny and,
um I forget the other guy's name, sorry" Fred replied. "Bill" the
younger journeyman shot back, not to feel left out. "I'm Gloria"
the ex-model now sales manager offered out. She looked at
Danny with a slight, sexy kind of flirtatious smile. Not that
Danny was movie star material mind you, but he had that rugged,
construction guy kind of appearance. At 6'2" and around 210
pounds, he was a big guy but not huge. His hands were calloused
and slightly scarred. Only when Danny was on vacation did the
dirt completely disappear from below his fingernails. His light
brown hair sticking out from under his ball cap matched his
mustache.
None of that really mattered as Danny was devoted to his wife of
twenty seven years and although he would be flattered by a smile
from a gorgeous women, that's as far as it would go. That and the
fact his wife looked 10 years younger than she was and could
hold her own in any beauty pageant. It was what attracted him to

her many years ago, her natural beauty, and of course her legs. Legs most men would die for. He had seen so many guys look for greener pastures and end up alone in smoke filled bars picking up whatever the younger, good looking dudes left behind.

"Did you have a contractor in here today dear?" asked Fred, Environmental Air Quality or something?" "Yes we did" Gloria said, "they come in once a year to check our air conditioning system, it's part of some corporate level, PM plan that I don't know much about. He gets up in the ceiling there on his ladder and monkeys around, looks at our thermostat and away he goes. I stamp the work order. No big deal. Honestly I think it is a waste of time and money but you know how big corporations are, so I don't ask any questions. "Where does he put up the ladder?" Bill asked out of the blue, trying not to sound like he was taking control of the questioning.

"Right up there" Gloria pointed, "where the ceiling tile is marked up a bit." Fred said, "what the heck, lets see what's up there." Bill got the ladder out of the back and they set it up under the marked tile. Danny went up with his flashlight and popped out the tile. Fred said he would be right back, he was going to go get a new ceiling tile to replace the dirty one, since they were right there. Danny peered into the area above the ceiling grid. "You sure it was here?" he asked her. "Yes, I'm quite sure, I had to walk around the ladder a few times to bring out some new merchandise."

"Well, unless I'm crazy, which is a distinct possibility, "Danny mused, " there is nothing up here but some wiring for the lights. I can't imagine what an air conditioning guy would be checking up here, I just don't get it."

Gloria exclaimed in a somewhat shocked tone, "you mean it is a scam, they have been ripping us off all this time?"

"I'm not sure what it is" Danny said, " I just don't get it." Fred returned with the new ceiling tile and Bill took it upon himself to replace it and also verify Danny's findings with his own eyes.. Fred asked, "well what did you see up there boys?" Danny said, "not much, I don't get it, lets head back to the basement and get a cup off coffee in your office." Yeah Fred retorted, "just maybe we will call this outfit and see what they are all about, just for kicks." Maybe it was nothing, maybe it was easily explained, but maybe it wasn't. Danny was thinking what Bill and Fred were, about the mysterious cardboard box in the air vent.

Chapter 3

On the way back to the maintenance office, Danny's cell phone rang. He recognized the number as one of his customers whom he was suppose to also service that day. It was a restaurant with an ice maker on the fritz. Restaurant owners went crazy when they ran out of ice. He would have to let the mystery at the mall wait. He told Bill to finish up here, clean up and throw out the old parts, hang around for 20 minutes and make sure everything was kosher. After that, Bill could finish up the rest of his service calls and go home. These guys didn't work by the clock, when they got done with what needed to be done, they went home. Sometimes they were done at 1 PM, others not till 10 PM. It was the nature of the business and they knew it well.

Meanwhile, a dark green, unmarked minivan pulled into the parking lot of the South Hills Village Mall complex. A man with an Environmental Air Quality jacket on emerged and proceeded to sign in at the office. He marked down the store as Lydia's. He returned to his van, removed a small cardboard box sealed in plastic and entered the back service entrance by the loading dock. He disappeared down the stairway towards the main mechanical rooms. On his way out of the mall he also made his customary stop at Lydia's., crawled up in the ceiling and played with the thermostat. He then got his work order stamped, signed out at the mall office and left.

As he pulled out of the lot he made a call on his cell phone to a long distance number. "This is JC, all done at South Hills. I have 4 more dispensers to place, the malls are getting a bit crowded now. I'm going to wrap it up for today. Will let you know when I get them all done."

"10-4" a raspy voice on the other end of the phone replied, "any problems so far?"

"Nada," he said, "all clear. I am too good for these clowns. Like taking candy from a baby. I do need to pick up another mask though. I'll grab it on the way out of town. I assume it will be at the usual place?"

"10-4" once again the raspy voice replied. "Just let me know when you are all done, and don't get too cocky you hear, that's how people get caught. If you do get caught, you are on your own, that's how it works, understand? If someone finds you wandering around the back hallways or mechanical rooms, you are lost, act dumb."

Though the man behind the raspy voice knew if his guy ever did get caught he would sing like a bird to avoid even one day of jail time.

"Sure, sure, I dig. I was thinking about that. Since I am taking all this risk we need to renegotiate my contract. I have been doing this for a long time for you guys. Besides it ain't easy travelling all around the country and staying in cheesy motels."

"You can stay wherever you want to JC, as long as it is out of the way and you don't attract attention to yourself, you know that. You stay in those flea bag joints to save money, don't BS me," the voice now getting irritated.

Well if you paid me more I could afford to............." "Not now, ya hear, we can discuss it later." and the phone went dead. "Cheap bastard JC said," and E .A. Q. rep pulled out onto the main highway.

Danny had the ice maker cranking out nice, solid cubes in no time. With the new LED diagnostics built into most circuit boards, troubleshooting was a no brainer for experienced guys like him. Danny had his usual free lunch, although he knew there was no such thing, and headed out. The restaurant owner owed Danny a substantial amount of money. He made payments when he could but often the payments didn't keep up with the repairs. So many smaller restaurants had fallen by the wayside, while large franchise places seemed to keep appearing all over the place. Times had changed. If you didn't have large corporate backing, owning a small restaurant got tougher and tougher. Danny wondered if the same would thing would happen to his industry some day. He felt if it did, he would get out, maybe joining Fred down in the warmer climate somewhere.

 Danny was done for the day. His next job was an installation of a rooftop air conditioning unit he had on hold until he could get all the subcontractors scheduled. He would need to line up the roofers, the crane guy, the actual unit and the electrician. That would take a couple days to get organized. Organization was the key in larger jobs like that. Having everyone and everything show up on time was critical to maximizing profits on bigger installation jobs. If one subcontractor didn't show, or the material didn't arrive as scheduled what you ended up with was a big waste of time and money. Since Danny had a small outfit it was much easier to keep on top of things like that. And he was very good at it. Over time he had compiled a very reliable list of subcontractors, not the cheapest guys in town mind you, but honest and fair.

On his way back to his tiny shop he picked up his cell phone and called Fred. "Hey Freddie, did you get a hold of that environmental outfit yet, just wondering?" Fred replied, "I tried but I can't find a local listing for them and Gloria has no idea either. She said that is handled on a corporate level and she is pretty much out of the loop on it. I checked, and the contractor listed his name as JC in the mall log so that is no help. I have to get up to the vestibule in front of Sears right now, major water leak. When I get that straightened out I am going to go check the security cameras and see if anything is on them." Then Danny heard Fred talking on his walkie-talkie, " Yeah Bob, I am on my way right now, the main shut off for that area is in the small janitors closet near the entrance to Sears, OK. Hey Danny, I gotta go." Good old Freddie, thought Danny. Puts out more fires than any fireman he ever knew.

Danny swung by his shop to get the mail and enter the invoice for the mall work into his computer. He would write up the invoice but hold it for a few days. He almost always did that on commercial service work. If something malfunctioned right after Danny fixed it or they had other issues in the area of the repair, it was wise to wait and be sure the problems were resolved before billing out the work. It was better to compile one large bill and include everything then to have to bill out a few smaller jobs for similar breakdowns. It just looked better. Danny had an ongoing PO, or purchase order, to use for the year with a "not to exceed" amount. It wasn't a guarantee that he had all the work there, a few other contractors were on file as well and of course they could call someone else in at any time. It certainly was a big plus to have the type of set up Danny had with them though. Mall personnel didn't like adding new vendors to their list. It took time and paperwork.

When Danny arrived at his shop he saw Bill's truck already there. He was picking up some parts for the job he was on. Bill told Danny he had done a temporary fix on the large boiler that heated the gigantic stone house of one of Danny's oldest customers, Mrs. Weiser.

Mrs. Weiser husband had died years ago and Danny was truly saddened at his passing.

They were one of his first customers when Danny went into business for himself. The house was in an older area of the city. Once a first class neighborhood with many high society and well to do residents, it had since given way to the big money boys shift out to the rich development in the nearby suburbs.

There still remained a few original home owners. Most houses had been bought and subdivided into rental properties catering to the nearby colleges and medical centers. And a few properties had been bought and renovated by younger, for lack of a better word, "yuppie" types who wanted to remain close to the city and its never ending activity. When Danny did work for any of them he noticed the thermostat during the winter months was routinely set at 60 degrees.

Heating a large, old house like that was not cheap, even if they did have a great job and drove a nice BMW, they still had heart failure when the gas bill came in the mail.

"You are taking care of Ms. Weiser I hope," Danny grinned to Bill. "I know she has grown somewhat kooky in her old age, but she is one of a kind in my book." "No problemo" replied Bill, "her boiler needs a new pressure regulator, I bypassed the old one and got her some heat until tomorrow. So I have to drain the entire system for that and, well, you know the deal. Plus, there are some bad shut off valves that need attending to, it will take most of the day, and that is if I am lucky." Danny knew it well, you never knew what you would run into. The older the house, the more likely to expect things to go bad. He had his share of horror stories ranging from burns to soakings to gas leaks to minor concussions. Part of the trade and a good reason to keep on your toes at all times.

Still, Danny liked working in the old homes. They were built to last, some of the craftsmanship used in their construction was long gone. New houses were usually put up in months. Most were cheaply made by builders who cared solely about money ando couldn't build a doghouse themselves. It was a sad state of affairs in Danny's mind. It just seemed as though everything was getting cheaper these days, I mean how far down could we go?

"She asked how you were Dan," Bill remarked. "I lied and said you were great, matter of fact, the greatest boss in the world." Bill was laughing out loud now. "Keep it up Billy boy," Dan shot back, " you will be head electric eel engineer on sewer cleaning detail in no time. A lot of my customers asked me why I don't do that anymore ya know? I could get that hooked up for you pretty easy. You got hired after those days but I could start that back up with no trouble, none at all." Bill just kept laughing and they both went back and forth a few times with the usual barbs and insults. A mutual respect allowed them the luxury of such encounters.

But Danny had started out in the business from the ground up, literally. Digging ditches for gas or water lines, cleaning out sewers and doing any job that would put food on the table. In those days, he couldn't afford to be picky. With his wife at home raising the kids and them relying solely on his income, Danny couldn't be picky at all. He often wondered if he had to do it all over again, if he would follow the same path, or would he opt for a career using his college education? He supposed most everyone in every line of work felt the same way and in the end he was ultimately satisfied in his choices. He had his own business, he was his own boss, they were well off, not rich mind you, but financially sound. The days of scrounging for extra money to get the kids clothes or pay bill collectors were long past, just a distant memory now. But through it all, they had handled it well, happy for what they had and happy for their wonderful family and friends. One thing they never fought over was money, no matter how little they had of it.

"Yeah ," Danny went on, letting the younger journeyman know just how good he had it. "My pop would send us on any job, in any neighborhood, we were not very discerning, not at all. I did my time in the trenches" a familiar slogan of Danny's, "and then some. You missed out on that fun buddy. Digging ditches in the dead of winter, when the winters were cold, not like now. –10 for days on end. Ya know, we didn't use fancy tools either, just a pick and shovel. The pick would bounce up off the frozen ground, we would hop in the truck to warm up, then go out for some more digging. A few times the customers would call the shop and complain that they were paying for us guys to sit in the truck, can you imagine? The jerks, not all customers mind you, some would invite you inside for hot coffee and such or give you a tip."

Danny continued on with a nostalgic gleam in his eye, "Did I ever tell you about the one time when I was working for my pop over the summer, when I was home from college? We were doing a gas line under a sidewalk, I was merely helping his full time plumbers, all I cared about was getting done, going home and going out drinking. I couldn't imagine being one of them plumbers with a full time job and family and responsibility that kept me tied down like that. Nope, I wanted no part of this business, I didn't want to end up like them, that's for sure." Bill had heard all this before but let Danny go on as he seemed to enjoy telling it so much.

"Well we had to repair the sidewalk after installing the new water line. One of the plumbers was Italian and everyone knows they are the best at concrete jobs. My dad always sent him on the cement stuff. It was an art to him, a secondary, mastered craft that was not as simple as it looked, not if you wanted it to look good and last.

His other plumber was your typical steam fitter.Both were big guys, with an attitude I could sense. I don't blame them for not

being fond of the bosses son tagging along. Not that I was
disrespectful or felt any superiority being the son of the guy who
signs their paychecks. I just wanted to stay out of their way, go
get parts or carry heavy objects around as needed. Soon it would
be time to go out partying with my buddies, in those days it was
easy to get served even if you were under age. So anyway, it's
hot as blazes and I am with these two burly pipe fitters, and the
one picks up an 80 pound bag of cement mix and slams it down
on the remaining part of the sidewalk, near the newly refilled
ditch. It breaks apart and he uses his shovel to mix it about.
Well, I think to myself, I can do that. They will see I am a tough
guy too. I grabbed another 80 pound bag of the dry cement
powder and lifted it up to slam it down too. As I heave it up over
my head, I hear one of them start to say something, but it all
happens in an instant. My bag goes right down on the opened pile
of dry cement and sends it flying up in the air, like baking flour
in a bakery. A cloud of dust enveloped the two, now really not so
thrilled with the bosses kid, plumbers. I mean it is on their face,
their clothes, in their hair, I'm sure up their nose, it was ugly."
All the one guy said was, "not good." I apologized all over the
place and they accepted. I think that was the last concrete job I
did with them. Well, it was for quite some time, anyway."
Danny was really into his story when the phone rang, it was Fred.
" Just wanted to let you know, the security tapes showed that JC
guy walking into the back stairway and heading down the
corridor towards the mechanical rooms. He didn't look like a guy
who was lost, not at all. He had some hand tools in a large pouch
and something in a plastic bag, hard to tell what it was. The tapes
also showed him returning without the plastic bag. From there he
headed out to the mall area. We don't have cameras all over the
place. I have no idea what he did after leaving the main corridor
or down near the mechanical areas. I can only assume he is the
one who put that cardboard box contraption in the duct. What do
you make of that Dan?"
Danny got serious, "I have no idea Fred, I wish I did."

With that, Danny told Bill of his conversation and the two of them kicked some ideas around. Perhaps it was some sort of duct testing, for air leaks? Not likely, was it some type of air flow test, did the guy use an infrared meter or ultra violet scanner or something up in Lydia's to test for...........they were really grabbing at straws now. Danny said when he got home he would log onto one of the HVAC, (heating, ventilating and air conditioning), internet sites he was a member of and ask them. There were all kinds of guys who belonged to these web site forums, guys from all over the country, all over the world even. You could ask anything in there and get some type of response. Surely one of them would have an idea. Bill said he was going to go online at the office computer and kill some time. His curiosity was peeked now. Bill was just the guy to find out too.

Bill Strathmore joined the army right out of high school. A smart kid who didn't apply himself to textbooks, he loved computers and was self taught in their use. The army promised him a career in the computer science field but as typically occurs, the recruiter lied a bit. Bill ended up in electronics and communications. It was OK but his love of computers was always there. After two years of electronics, Bill applied for an opening in computer science and was accepted. He learned the real nature of computers and ended up in the code breaking division at the Pentagon. After that, Danny never did find out what happened but Bill was honorably discharged and sent packing.

Bill was so upset he swore off computers and went to trade school for heating and air conditioning, something he had done for one summer helping his older cousin. Bill mainly took courses in the controls end of the field and studied hard. The new energy management systems and commercial controllers were very similar to computers and he picked it up easily. On his graduation from trade school, Bill called almost every air conditioning contractor in the phone book asking if they were hiring. A few said yes they were, and to send them a resume. Bill wrote up his resume, which was very impressive, and got some professional looking copies made at Kinkos. Armed with the written history of his background he headed out to pursue a new career. Bill stopped for lunch at one of the many fast food, greasy hamburger joints. He had some school loans now and a young baby daughter besides. Eating cheap would be a daily occurrence for him from now on. As he sat down with his tray full of fried cholesterol he noticed a guy at the next table wearing typical work clothes with an embroidered patch on the shirt. On that patch he made out the words, air conditioning. What a coincidence he thought, he struck up some small talk and mentioned he was just now on his way to give his resume out to some HVAC contractors in hopes of landing a job. Danny Edwards took off his ball cap, pushed his light brown curly hair back off his forehead and said, "if you are really looking for a job in this crazy field, you just found it." Bill gave Danny one of his resumes since he had the fancy things right out in his car, and it only added to his credibility. Honestly, at this point, in the middle of a hot spell and Danny already booked with work and more jobs coming in every week, he probably would have hired Bill regardless of his impressive background. And so it began, Bill learning the mechanical end of the trade while using his computer/electronics background to help his boss spread out into a new, more technology driven part of the industry. Danny was an older guy who knew his way around controls and computers some, but not like Bill. In no time at all Bill was the main man as far as that went. It allowed the small outfit to move into a larger market where hourly rates were often in the $150/hr range. Bill was well compensated for his efforts. It was a situation that worked well for both of them. They still did the simple stuff too though, there was good money in that as well. You never knew when you would need to go back to your roots in this business, and knowing how things worked from the ground up was essential. Danny often wondered why Bill picked air conditioning work, I mean with his background, he could have chosen several career paths, ones that didn't require a strong back and coming home dirty.

Bill would always say, as much he liked computers and such, he couldn't picture himself in a cubical all day long deciphering code. In the army it was OK, an adventure so to speak. But in the corporate world, well, lets just say Bill's favorite movie was Office Space, a cult comedy about a bored computer programmer who ends up doing construction work after he and his buds fail at scamming their employer out of large sums of money, a fraction of a penny at a time.

One thing Danny knew from his conversations with Bill, and seeing him action on a keyboard, there weren't too many people who could make a computer do things Bill Strathmore could. Many guys could point and click their way around, following prompts from software programs and organizing data, but Bill really knew what made them tick. There were a couple times, over a few too many draft beers Bill would go into some detail about his job at the Pentagon. What Danny heard convinced him that Bill could most likely hack into any computer network or web site should he have the desire to do so. But bill kept those talents under wraps. His unexplained, yet rapid departure from the army had taught him to keep his curiosity and creative skills locked away in his internal hard drive. And there they remained, in a subfolder but not formatted.

As Danny left for home, Bill logged on the www using the computer at the shop. It had a DSL connection through the phone company and was not as fast his cable modem at home. He was used to the speed of his home system and got frustrated waiting for the computer at the shop to respond. First he did a Google search for Environmental Air Quality Inc. And of course that brought up literally millions of hits with the most relevant being that of an EPA web site on air quality. He spent some time working his way through the long list and tried different headings to narrow it down. No luck, if it was there it would take days to find it using search engines. Then he decided to enter different web addresses such as www.Environmentalairqualityinc.com , and www.eaqinc.com and so on. All he located was one listing that said domain name being held for use. Other than that no listing for the company. That was odd, in a day when almost every company has a web address of some sort, why nothing on a company that has contracts for major retailers like Lydia's? OK then, lets check out Lydia's, what the hell. That was easy to find and had your usual major retailer web site. You could buy clothes on it, find stores in your area, contact them for employment opportunities, check out specials and peruse their newest fashions. Bill clicked on the store's history icon. Seemed it was founded by Lydia herself, imagine that. Once a small store in New Jersey, it has spread throughout the country in less than 10 years. It listed almost 150 branch outlets in every major mall. They must be doing something right Bill thought. Bill did some further digging and followed some links here and there and was about to log off when he noticed that Lydia's was actually owned by a large drug manufacturing company, Rycon-Rx. Corporation. Not unusual at all. Many large corporations owned smaller companies for various reasons as a way to diversify or perhaps simply for a tax write off . He still thought it odd a clothier was owned by a large drug conglomerate. Oh well, time to get home, maybe he would do some more digging at night, on his home computer. Oops, wait, my daughter is in a play at her preschool tonight, can't miss that, Bill remembered. He locked up the shop and headed out, now thinking about other things more relevant to him, the play, his soon to be wife, what was for dinner and getting back to Mrs. Weisers the next day to straighten out that big, old boiler. The incident at the Valley View mall now faded from his memory, he would work on it later, if he ever got the time. His stomach growled and he stopped by the grocery store and picked up some fresh steaks for dinner. Not too many nice days left to grill out he thought, not many at all. The leaves were blowing off the trees as the change of seasons drew near. Meanwhile, Danny was already at home checking out the various HVAC related web forums. He posted what he saw that morning and asked if anyone had ever seen anything like that or heard of that company.

No one had, but he would give it time. People came and went on those sites, perhaps in a day or so someone would have some experience with them and post a reply. He talked about some other things with his web buddies until he heard his wife, Francesca Elizabeth whom everyone called Liz, coming home from work. She had stayed late for a meeting and came in the door railing on about some new procedures the administration had just laid out.

"All they do is dream up more stuff for us to do, " she bitched, "calling parents every other week, filling out new lesson plan forms, new security procedures and all kinds of ridiculous junk. I can see why the older teachers get disgusted," she went on." Instead of dealing with the real issues like kids fighting and yelling back at us disrespecting us and swearing in the hallways and pulling all sorts of crap, they have meetings telling us to make sure the back doors are closed and locked at all times and everyone has to use the main entrance from now on. How ridiculous is that?

If someone wants to get in that school it would be very simple. Hell, everyone there I know just wants to get out of it." Liz laughed. Danny agreed. "Most of this so called high security after 9/11 is a waste.

If some terrorist really wanted to blow something up, it is unlikely any of this nonsense would stop them.

If you wanted to stop terrorism, quit letting anybody and everybody into this country," Danny now on a rant. Although if that had been the case a few hundred years ago, Danny would probably be fixing furnaces in Ireland. But things were different now, more complicated, more confusing. He thought of that guy at the mall and how simple it had been for him to walk in and out of the back hallways and mechanical rooms.

He told Liz about it and she shrugged it off.

"Could be anything," Dan, "don't jump the gun, I know you like conspiracy theories and all but…"

Danny ranted on a bit more.

"There is no way to assure everything was safe, no way possible. In the end, all we do is just inconvenience ourselves into believing it is. Much as we can try, there is just no way to stop someone from doing something terrible in a country that offers as much freedom as ours. The best defense is for everyone to keep their eyes and ears open, and don't be afraid to get involved."

Chapter 4

It was after midnight and the train was late. Danny tossed and turned in his bed. Liz was fast asleep as usual. Her early mornings gave way to 10 pm bedtimes, dozing off while watching the local news.

Danny would stay up awhile longer and have a late night snack while channel surfing through mainly the large array of Science, History, or Discovery programs. He had seen most of them already but occasionally a new one would pop up. Well at least there was something good about so many cable channels he would force himself to admit. When his eyelids got heavy he would make his way up the stairs and hit the sack. During the busy times when Danny worked 10-12 hour days, falling asleep was no problem. But sometimes during the slow periods doing only one or two calls a day, he still had energy to burn long after the sun set. He had been up early this day, getting to the mall way before it opened but had taken a small catnap after dinner. Now he was in bed but his mind was racing. It was no use, no train to help him either, where was it? He went back downstairs and decided to check on the internet air conditioning forum he had been on previously. Maybe someone had posted a response to his question about that EAQ outfit. He logged on under his user name, his saved password and cookie recognition took him quickly into the HVAC-Talk forum. The main page of the forum had a small listing at the bottom of it showing all the member's who were online at that time. To be precise, it listed their screen names, or handles, chosen by members to post under. Many screen names were simply for fun but several referred to the type of specific business they were in such as FreezeKing or LowTemp. You could assume these guys were heavy into the refrigeration end of things. If your name was Control-Dr or EMS-Dude, you were probably involved in energy management or commercial controls. Often guys used parts of their surnames or just made stuff up for no real reason. It gave everyone a certain anonymity, although if you wanted you could list a profile on the web site. A profile that held your true identity, location and experience in the industry. He seldom read the names of members currently online unless he was looking for someone specific, perhaps to find out about a certain job they were on or maybe to ask how the guy's family was doing. Danny had been a member of the HVAC based internet site for over 5 years. He had made a lot of cyber friends and many of them had even met on occasion. In recent years some of them held a yearly get together or "convention" as they liked to refer to it. It was more of a two-day party with each member taking a turn hosting the event in his city. The number of attendees grew each year, and many were anxious to get their name on the list to be the next host city. Danny and Liz always attended.

Danny was ready to jump from the main page into one of the categorys and eventually to the area where he had posted his remarks about the mystery company and the cardboard box. Then something caught his eye, a members name on the bottom of the main page. A member who was online now but one Danny had never noticed before, JC-EAQ. He clicked on the name and checked on his profile, nothing there. Not that unusual, many guys liked to keep to themselves on the internet. They didn't want any personal information put out there, information that could be used for someone else's personal gain. With identity theft and countless scams who could blame them.

What was unusual was the registration date of JC-EAQ. That was something not controlled by the member, it was just marked down under their name when they first registered, as was the number of posts by that member.

JC-EAQ had been on this site for three years and change. His total post count was zero. He was what many called a lurker. And he was online right now. "I wonder" Danny mused out loud, "I wonder."

He went to the general discussion area, one where members could discuss things not necessarily related to the air conditioning industry. It was there he posted his previous query about the box and EAQ. Except for a few of his buddies making wise ass remarks about Danny drinking too early in the morning or possible flashbacks from his misbehaving during his college years, no one had heard of them, or any cardboard box that periodically smokes and disintegrates when touched. That was hard to believe.

It was dark in that mechanical room, maybe his eyes had tricked him. No, the others had seen it too and he was thankful for that. Something was going on, something odd.

Danny started a new topic heading, one easily seen on the main page under general discussion section. It read, "Hey JC-EAQ, do I know you?"

He waited and there was no reply. The guy could be in another area of the forum, reading up on technical matters or business advice. Danny would go to one of those sections and kill some time. He returned to his new topic and there was a response. It was from one of his long time cyber buds, CoolCat. It said, "Hey, DanTheMan," Danny's simple yet relative screen name, "I think we got a lurker here. They bug me" CoolCat continued. "If you are going to read in here the least you could do is speak up once in awhile, know what I mean?" "Yeah" Danny typed back, "I don't get it, this guy has been in here for over three years and not one single post, and it isn't like he just faded away, he was online tonight when I logged on., weird."

"CoolCat replied, "I saw your other post about the cardboard box and that company, Environmental Air Quality or something, any relation to this?"

"I'm not sure yet,"" Danny typed back "there is another coincidence here, this guys name being JC. I'm not going to get into it now though."

"Hang loose" CoolCat shot back, "gotta go, c ya on the flip side" "Goodnight Cool, " Danny responded, and with that he went back to the main page and saw "JC-EAQ" was offline already. Had he seen Danny's post about him?

Danny slid the chair back under the computer desk, hit the lights and headed back upstairs. He quietly crept back into their California king water bed so as not to wake Liz. She stirred, turned over and said something under her breath about school. "I wonder what she is dreaming about," Danny grinned to himself.

In short order, Danny was in the midst of his own night time adventures, so bizarre yet somehow so real.

Danny was up early, noticing the lack of light as autumn fast approached. Soon it would be winter, long, dark and cold. The holiday season was always nice, and the first few snowfalls were beautiful in their own way. The majesty of newly fallen snow, a dark, clear night where you could see the Milky Way galaxy and the smell of winter in the air were things Danny loved. Shoveling the white stuff and getting stuck in snowdrifts were not as wonderful however. After the holidays were over and the newness of the winter wonderland had grown commonplace, all Danny wanted was for it to all go away. Bring back the sunlight, the warmth, the flowers and the leaves on the trees. Of course these things were appreciated much more so by the fact they had not been around for some time. In the back of his head, Danny knew that and in all honesty he enjoyed the seasons and the changes they brought. It is what kept him living well north of the equator, that and the fact he couldn't imagine not living in the area he was accustomed to. Danny's cell phone rang, it was Bill, "I am going to get what I need and get over to old lady Weisers" he said. "Should be fun, I'll let you know how it goes. I should have it wrapped up by this afternoon."

"OK" Danny replied, "let me know if you run into anything over there, that is one, big old house. Just touching some of that stuff is asking for trouble. Be careful, she is too old for any excitement like water gushing out of her ceilings or gas explosions," Danny laughed. " I am going to get that rooftop job moving, don't want to be doing that in the snow, and our daylight is running low too. Talk to you later."

Danny grabbed another cup of coffee and got out his rolodex of phone numbers. He would confirm the scheduling dates and make sure everyone was on board. After that he had a few service calls that could wait, he went back online and logged into the HVAC forum. Not much new since last night he guessed, but low and behold, JC-EAQ was back in the site. There was no response from him, just lurking again.

Shortly after Danny logged on, he noticed JC-EAQ had logged out. Danny decided he would sic Bill on this one, just to see if he could come up with an IP address for this JC-EAQ guy or something.

The office phone line rang, it was Bob Baylack from Chemical Imagery Group, a customer of Danny's.

"Hey Dan, we got a problem with the air conditioning unit in the microscope lab," Bob said. "Can you get down here and take a look, it's kind of a critical situation. We have some new instruments being tested and some potential clients in town as well. Would appreciate it if you could schedule us in for sometime today" Bob continued. "Not a problem" said Danny, "I will be there sometime this morning."

Danny loved customers like that. Top shelf companies with money to spend when it needed spending.

They never called anyone but him. On bigger jobs his was the only estimate they got. But Danny didn't abuse that trust, he was very fair with all his customers. He had worked hard to get where he was and although he deserved to make good money in the process, he knew not to take advantage either.

He finished calling his subcontractors and the supplier of the new air conditioning unit he was to install later that week. Everything was set for Friday morning, weather permitting. The roofers would be there, the electrician and the crane company with the new unit in tow. And of course he and Bill would be ready for action as well.

Not that there was a whole lot for them to do that first day, all they had to do was make sure everything ran smooth. If, by the end of the day the new unit was in place, the roof was sealed and, as he liked to joke, "nobody died in the process," than it was a good day.

Danny took one last coffee for the road and headed out. He called Bill on his cell and asked how it was going at Mrs. Weisers. "Just fricking great" Bill said. "I snapped the old fitting where the water line goes into the boiler. I think I can clean it up and get some new ones piped in there, but it's going to take awhile. My pants are soaking wet too, damn, down in that old, hot, nasty basement. And when I go outside it's like 50 degrees, I hope I don't get sick, it's that time of year"

"How is Mrs. Weiser handling all that," Danny chuckled.

"She is making me some hot soup and insists I change my clothes, she says she has some old things of her late husband that should fit me. I can picture myself wearing his wool slacks and a pair of his leather slippers, as if."

Danny was laughing out loud now, "well just be nice, she means well, humor her"

" I know Dan," Bill said, " she reminds me of my grandmother, they don't make them like that anymore."

"Well anyway," Danny went on, "If you get done in time, later this afternoon, there is something I want you to look at, on the internet. Maybe we can meet at the shop and I'll show you."

"You mean that EAQ company we were looking into yesterday" Bill replied, "I checked em out some and couldn't come up with anything obvious on them. Of course I haven't really tried yet, I was only on in first gear. When I want to put my skills in overdrive it's quite a different story you know."

"Oh yeah Billy boy, I know, I know quite well. We just may need you to get into overdrive on this one, I'll tell you more about it later, when I see you. Now go dry off and have some tea with Mrs. Weiser, if she starts hitting on you be careful, I think her dead husband still roams around there, down in the basement, by the boiler." Danny was cracking himself up now. He could just see Bill in the old wool slacks of the late Mr. Weiser, having tea and petting Mrs Weiser's dog, Harry, named after her dearly departed husband.

A phone rang in a back office of a storefront in New Jersey. A raspy voice answered, "Yeah what's up?"

"JC here, I think we may have a little problem." was the reply. " I told you not to get cocky, damn it." the voice angrily retorted. "If you get caught we will hang you out to dry, understand?"

"It wasn't anything I did, trust me. I followed the same procedure. No one saw me, no one said anything, in and out. But some guy is asking about me on the internet site I use to gather information for my job. He wants to know about our company too. I'm not sure, he might just be trolling me for fun."

The voice shot back, "How did he know who you were? Why would he single you out? What is going on JC, don't make this any worse, if you did something dumb lets hear it……..now."

"I didn't do anything dumb, now get off my back. I'm not in the mood for your accusations right now. I am the one whose neck is on the line here, it will be me who gets caught and prosecuted, not you." JC was getting defensive. He would not tell his "employer," so to speak, about using his initials or the EAQ reference on the web site. They were untraceable anyway, and he just couldn't resist using them.

Maybe it was his little way of showing off how smart he was. JC was indeed cocky and in the end it would lead to his downfall. The raspy voice continued in a louder tone now.

"You are well paid my friend, very well paid. You knew there was some risk and you accepted it. I'm not going into all that again, perhaps you weren't the right man for the job."

JC now trying to calm down his cohort, "Listen, relax man, like I said, probably nothing. I'll monitor it and handle the situation. Anyway, besides the boxes, I need some more masks. I am going to pick them up at the same place tomorrow morning, I assume they will be there?"

"They will be there." click the line went dead, the conversation abruptly terminated.

Danny pulled into the lot of the Chemical Imagery Group and checked in at the main desk. He had his tool bag and his gauges with him. It was not a formal check in, no name tags, no high tech security in this place. He was buzzed in the front door and Bob was notified of his arrival. They were a newer company with an innovative product. They liked keeping things low profile. While Danny waited for Bob to meet him one of the engineers strolled by and remarked, "Hey Dan, more A/C problems?"

"You know it chief." Danny replied. "Back in the microscope room I understand. Not cooling very well and some big shots in town?"

"Oh right" the horn rimmed PhD of chemistry agreed. "It's blowing warm air around, the scopes might melt down" he laughed.

"Just what exactly do you do with those things?" Danny asked. He had heard them described before but didn't pay much attention to the detail.

"In a nutshell, we can use chemical imaging to detect any known substance. We can do it in far less time and with greater accuracy than any other procedures currently being used by other similar companies.

For example we can detect Anthrax in just a few hours, other labs can take days for positive test results."

Bob came around the corner, "Glad you got here so quick, I'll show you what is going on."

Danny and Bob went back to the microscope area. "See what I mean, getting warm back here," and then Bob had to go attend to other duties.

Danny evaluated the system, low on refrigerant charge. He found some oil on a fitting and knew that was where the leak was. Most likely the only one, he hoped. He repaired the leak, recharged the unit and the temperature started dropping again. The microscopes would be cool, the big shots in town would be impressed, Bob Bavlack would be happy and as a result, Danny would be satisfied he had done his part in all of it. That's what it was all about, that and making good money in the process.

Danny returned to his shop to get the mail, Bill's truck was outside.

Bill was at the computer, wearing a pair of loose fitting wool slacks.

"Compliments of Mrs. Weiser, I presume" Danny laughed.

"Yep, real stylish, huh? I have to keep extra work pants in the truck from now on." Bill moaned.

"I always do, and socks and shirts and even towels, you will learn" Danny grinned.

"So is her boiler fixed? Did she tip you? How is Harry?"

"Yes, yes and Harry needs a female companion I think." Bill said.

"You know how many times he jumped up and started grinding on my leg?"

"Well, I lost count after five but I think when I finally yelled, I ain't your bitch ya mangy flea bag, now get the hell out of here, Mrs Weiser must of heard and took the hint. She called Harry upstairs and locked him in a room, Thank God."

Danny was smiling, "Did her dead husband show up, he likes it down in the boiler room. Maybe he didn't like how you talked to his namesake and caused that pipe to break on you, ever think of that.

"No, that never occurred to me," Bill sarcastically replied. "I can't wait to get home and burn these ugly pants, my thighs are itching like a mother."

Danny peered over Bill's shoulder and saw he was surfing web sites. "I couldn't find anything on that EAQ outfit except that one of the names I entered said the domain was being held," Danny said, "nobody on any of the HVAC web sites has heard of them either, strange. I did manage to check out Lydia's web page and nothing unusual there. Well, one thing stuck out, Lydia's is owned by a large drug manufacturer, but these days with so many big corporations owning smaller companies...."

His voice trailing off as he watched Bill's fingers racing over the keyboard.

"Yeah, I already saw that but look here," Bill exclaimed, "Rycon-Rx has many subsidiaries, and besides Lydia's, they also own a small company called, Melcher Corp. And digging a little deeper, Melcher owns,' he paused for effect.…..."Environmental Air Quality."

They both stared at the computer screen for a few seconds.

"That's quite a coincidence isn't it?"

Dan remarked. "I think it's more than just a coincidence," Bill shot back.

"So do I," Danny agreed, "so do I."

Bill closed out the web sites and said he was heading home to change his clothes. He would work on this later, at his house, using the faster cable modem his computer was hooked up to. As he headed out he mumbled, "there has to be some connection here, maybe laundering money, I don't know yet, but I got this feeling something is rotten in Denmark."

Bill loved stuff like this, corporate scandals, conspiracy theories, urban legends. At the Pentagon he spent long hours delving into such matters, and he was pretty damn good at it too.

Danny pulled into his driveway, still thinking about the whole matter. He shut off the truck and went inside, He checked the HVAC web sites, nothing new on his inquiry's. He heard Liz upstairs talking on the phone to her mother. He went upstairs past Liz, still talking on the phone. He could smell something good cooking. He continued up to the 3rd floor, got out of his work clothes, took a shower and sat down on the bed. He was getting a headache and felt somewhat achy. His nose was running a little and he felt a wave of exhaustion come over him. He took some Tylenol.

"Come on down, dinners ready," Liz yelled up the stairs, "it's going to get cold."

Danny made his way down to the table, "looks good" he said. He clicked the news on the smaller TV they had in the corner of the kitchen. "I think I'm coming down with something," he said. "Feels like a cold."

"There are a lot of kids sick in school too" Liz replied, "I wish they would stay home, all they do is come in and cough all over everyone." As they ate and watched the news Danny remarked, "yeah it's that time of year I guess, look at all the commercials for cold pills and such, unreal. I bet drug companies are thrilled people get sick, they would go broke if they didn't."

"So true" Liz agreed, "just like you get thrilled when someone's furnace breaks, huh?"

She was grinning as she said, "making money off others misery, the American way."

"I guess you could look at it that way," Danny laughed. "I'm still working on that incident at the mall you know." he told Liz.

"You are too much honey, you know that?" She laughed. They cleaned up after dinner and went in to watch a movie on HBO. Their older daughter came home from work, the only child left in an otherwise empty nest. She made herself something to eat then came in to watch the rest of the movie with her folks. After the movie, Danny took a double dose of Nyquil and hit the sack in the spare bedroom, he didn't want Liz to catch his cold. He fell asleep way before the train came rumbling along.

Chapter 5

Danny awoke early with a full blown cold. His nose was running and it was hard to breathe lying down. He looked at the clock, 6 AM. He took some Sudafed cold pills and turned on his coffee pot.

"I am staying home today" he mumbled under his breath, "screw it."

Liz came down all ready for school, "I would give you a kiss goodbye but," she hesitated.

"No, stay away from me, you don't want to get the plague too," Danny said. She hurried down the basement stairs and Danny heard the garage door open and then close a few seconds later.He looked out the window and saw her speed off.

"She drives too damn fast."

He turned on the tube and sat down with his coffee, covered with a small blanket they kept on the back of the couch.

"Severe cold and flu season expected this year" the newscaster on CNN reported. "New strains of Asian flu are expected to hit the US later this year," it went on. "The US also expects a shortage of flu vaccine. The elderly and those with health problems as well as health care workers should get their shots early."

"I guess the rest of us will just have to suffer" Danny mused, "great."

The Sudafed was kicking in and Danny felt slightly better. He checked his schedule. Things were slowing down now.

His business usually did this time of year, between seasons. He still planned on doing the rooftop installation later in the week, by then he would be OK. No matter how sick Danny was, if it was really necessary, he went to work, that's how it was. A short time later the phone rang. "Hey Dan," it was Bill. "Can I put off those calls for today, I got a hell of a cold."

"You too?" Danny said, "Yeah, you sound bad, I know how you feel, no problem, they can wait."

"Good," Bill said, "I'm going to work on that little mystery, just for kicks. I'll let you know if I find out any info on those outfits. Something tells me there is a connection. Not sure what or why but there is." His days at the Pentagon gave him a certain skepticism about such matters. "Achoo," Bill sneezed into the receiver, "crap, I'll be around if you really need me, OK?"

"Get some rest, the calls can wait." Danny hung up and went back to watching the news, alternating between sipping his coffee and blowing his nose.

The dark green minivan pulled up to the self storage area. The driver entered the code at the entrance gate and it rose up. He made his way back to one of the individual units and unlocked the door. He snatched up the rest of the small boxes sealed in

plastic and grabbed the last of the larger packages and made his
way out. On his navigation system in the van he looked up some
directions. "Center City Mall, take route 48 to the expressway
and then get off at the 4th street exit," the driver's voice said
aloud. "Yeah, I remember now, and the mechanical rooms are on
the 1st floor, I think." To be sure he entered some numbers on his
navigation system and it changed, showing the original blueprints
of the mall. "Yep, there it is, under the food court."
He located the particular work order for the location and put it in
his jacket's pocket. He took a sealed box and small mask, which
he got from the larger box, and buried them in the bottom of his
rather large tool bag. With that, he pulled the van out onto the
main road.

Bill's computer was taking him to places that only someone with
his ability could. He tracked IP addresses and snuck in some back
doors that were off limits. A connection between Rycon-Rx,
Lydia's and EAQ was more than apparent. He had blocked his
own computer and was operating in a stealth mode, so as not be
found out. As he did some more digging into Melcher Corp. he
found a lot of communication between them and EAQ. It didn't
seem to just be a larger company owning a smaller one. They had
daily communications back and forth. Melcher Corp listed an
address in New Jersey. On Mapquest Bill located it and used
Google to get a satellite image of the area. "What the hell," he
muttered. "What a dumpy, run down section of town. Why would
that company be located there? Unless these images were
outdated or they moved?"
He logged on one his web forums, made up of mostly ex-military
guys. One of his old buddies was from New Jersey and a regular
on the site. He posted in the main discussion area. "Hey Rambo"
the guys handle, "Can you do me a favor?"
Then thinking the better of it, he stopped there. "Well I think I
better e-mail you this one, so check your mail and let me know."
He logged out of the forum and sent an encrypted e-mail to
Rambo. "Can you check out this address for me? It is suppose to

be Melcher Corp, and seemingly a large company. The Google satellite view shows it to be in a real shit hole area of town. Can you take a digital pic of it and shoot it back here for me. Thanks, bro."

Bill then went back into stealth and continued on with his investigation. Try as he might, he could not find any physical location for EAQ. And that seemed odd. No shop, no address, nothing. "How can a contractor operate like that?" he wondered. Even if you worked out of your house and kept a low profile, something would show up.

His cell phone rang. The called ID showed it to be a blocked number. He answered, "Hello," thinking it to be a wrong number or pesky tele-marketer. "Bill, is this Bill Strathmore?" The raspy voice asked. "It might be, who wants to know?" Bill shot back. The line went dead. The caller was gone.

Danny picked up the phone and called the Valley View Mall, he got switched down to the maintenance department. A voice unfamiliar to Danny answered, "Hello, Jim Woods."

Then Danny remembered him, he was the night shift guy. By now it was 8:30 and his shift was over by then. "Hey Jim, this is Danny Edwards, how are you? Is Freddie around?"

"Naw, he called in sick so I have to hang around until they can get a replacement for him. Can I help you? The unit you worked on is purring like a kitten by the way."

At this point Danny didn't want to go into anything regarding the cardboard box incident so he just replied, "No, that's OK, I'll talk to him later, glad the system is up and running. Anything comes up, don't hesitate to call."

"OK Dan, will do, thanks for the quick service, we appreciate it, bye."

Danny hung up and went back to watching the TV. More drug commercials filled the airways. Between them and the lousy daytime programming Danny was restless. He closed his eyes to try and nap but all that coffee, along with the Sudafed prevented it.

The cell phone rang in the dark green minivan. "Yeah" the EAQ rep answered.

"I think you were right about that little problem. We may have to deal with it sooner than later," the raspy voice continued. "I may need you to coordinate efforts out there in this regard, since you are familiar with the area. I'll keep you informed as needed. Hold up on placing any more containers but don't check out of the motel yet, hang around for a day or so, I don't care how you kill time but just stay there. Got it?"

"I got it but what's up, exactly?" JC was curious how the internet site questions had worked their way back to the home office.

"Lets just say someone has been snooping around, someone who is very good at it too. And it must have something to do with the guy you were worried about, on that web site. It's too much of a coincidence. By the way, using your own initials on there was pretty stupid JC, especially combined with the EAQ. Yes, I saw it long ago, and let it go. That's your problem, not mine, in time you may have to deal with it."

"Hey" JC retorted, "I get paid per diem here you know. If I can't place anymore boxes then what? I am already on my way. I am going in and put this one down then I'll head back to the motel and wait." "You are a real jackass JC, you know that," the voice replied.

Click, the conversation was over.

Danny finally dozed off but the cold pills kept his mind racing. His dreams were intense, and so real.

He saw a guy in an EAQ coat, over at Mrs. Weisers, he was all wet and told Danny he was married to her. Bill was there too, lying in an upstairs bedroom on a hospital cot. He had a nurse with him and a doctor who told Danny that Bill didn't have long to live. Danny was then getting on a roller coaster, with his wife Liz, only when he looked again, it wasn't Liz, it was someone else. Someone he didn't know at all. She looked like the store manager at Lydia's. The young kid in charge of the ride said, "make sure your seat belts are fastened and keep your arms inside the ride at all times."

The roller coaster started up a big hill, as it made it's way over the top, Danny could see below that the tracks ended at the bottom, into a lake. He screamed as it raced downward, faster and faster.

His entire body jumped off the couch. He was suddenly wide awake, another ad for cold medication was on the TV. "Jesus Christ," Danny said as he shut off the TV, "that's enough of that shit."

He laid back down on the couch and fell fast asleep, that is until the phone rang shortly after 11 am.

The phone blared with its same annoying ring. Danny almost let it go, figuring the machine would get it. He needed to get a drink anyway, so he grabbed it on his way into the kitchen. "D & E mechanical," he answered trying to sound professional, though he felt like crap. "Hey Dan, Fred Ward here," sounding as bad as Danny. "I got a call from a friend of mine at the Center City Mall."

"Man, you sound awful, are you as sick as I am?" Danny coughed into the phone.

"I think so, nasty cold, must be going around." And Fred went on, "after that incident at our place the other day I put the word out to some other facility managers I know, at some of the other malls. I asked them to be on the lookout for a contractor with the name Environmental Air Quality or EAQ. If they saw them around to give me call and if they could, keep an eye on them. My buddy Jack McBride, down at Center City, just called me on my cell, seems that guy just checked into the mall. He registered under the name JC. What do you think, you want to take a ride over there?"

"Yeah, as bad I feel right now I am up for it, I'll meet you there ASAP. Danny took another Sudafed and got dressed.

He heated up the last cup of coffee remaining in the pot. He had to hurry, he knew the guy would be in and out of there in less

than an hour. He decided route 48 would have a lot of traffic and all the lights on that road would take too much time.
He took a shortcut on a windy road that bypassed it. It went through a lot of neighborhoods and eventually through a single lane tunnel, but with any luck he would make it to the mall in about 20 minutes.

JC finished placing the box in the main air handler in the mall's mechanical area. He simply opened an access door to the large unit, put on his mask and some disposable gloves, removed the cardboard box and set it inside the unit. All the while he looked over his shoulder and made sure he was alone, no security cameras down there, mostly they are all up in the shopping areas. When JC was done he took off his gloves and the plastic wrap that had held the box and put them in another small plastic bag. He then took off his mask and put both items back in his tool bag. A he left the mechanical area, a maintenance man who worked for the mall came around the corner and saw him. 'Can I help you?" the guy asked.
"Well, I guess. I have a work order here for service at Lydia's," JC quickly pulling out the work order from his jacket pocket. "I think I made a wrong turn somewhere."
"You sure did," the uniformed employee remarked, never bothering to check the work order. "Lydia's is up on the second level, down at the end by Macy's" At this point Jack McBride came down the hall and saw them both.
"OK, thanks man," and JC headed down the hallway towards the entrance doors to the mall.

Jack trailed behind the guy in the EAQ coat, keeping out of view. Occasionally the sneaky contractor would look back over his shoulder but thought nothing of others making their way through the back maze of staircases and hallways. As the EAQ jacket disappeared through 2 swinging doors and out into the main shopping area, Jack saw that he pulled something out of his tool bag and pitched it in a trash can located just before the large doors. A small item that would normally disappear under mounds of trash never to be given a second thought. But not today. Today that little miscue would be quite significant.

Jack retrieved it from the trash, looking at it strangely but not unwrapping it. He put it in his pocket and followed the intruder awhile longer. He paused at a pretzel stand watching the man enter Lydia's. The EAQ rep got out his work order, showed it to the store manager and got the stepladder all stores kept in their back room. Nothing seemed unusual as he checked the thermostat, looked above the ceiling and appeared to be adjusting something. He got the work order signed and headed back down to sign out at the management office. There he would return the guest pass, which gave him access to off limit areas, including the roof, and sign out marking down what time of day it was. It was normal procedure for all

private contractors who worked there.

Some malls were stricter than others, especially the newer ones. Many of the old ones you could walk in, go the store, do your work and just leave. Unless you needed special access somewhere, no one was the wiser.

Danny pulled into the parking lot of Center City Mall. He headed back by the loading dock looking for Fred. Then he saw it. The dark green minivan. He recognized it by the tinted windows. It was parked all by itself about 150 feet from the back entrance. The driver could have easily parked closer, why didn't he? Danny pulled up a few spaces over from the van. He cautiously looked around. That area of the parking lot was empty save their 2 vehicles. The back windows were tinted but not the front, by law you couldn't tint the front windshield. He meandered over and looked inside. For a work truck the thing sure was empty. Usually contractors trucks were packed full of stuff, ladders, tools, parts and all kinds of junk. There were some small boxes Danny noticed in the back of the van. He went around the back and put his face up against the window for a better look. They were covered in a dark plastic, they looked the size of the one they had found on Monday, at the Valley View Mall. "Now what

the heck is this?' Danny mumbled to himself. He backed up a
couple feet and saw an out of state license plate, from New Jersey
no less. "Figures" he thought out loud, not sure why it figured but
at this point it just seemed to fit right in.
"Hey, Can I help you dude?" A voice yelled from behind him.
Danny turned and saw the same guy he had seen on Monday,
coming towards him at a fast pace, with his EAQ jacket on.
"Oh, no, I was just making some calls from my truck here, I don't
like to do that while I'm driving.
Too many accidents you know. Better to pull over first. Nice van,
what year is it?" Trying to make up something on the spot. "I
prefer a full size truck for this line of work," Danny pointing to
his 1 ton Chevy van with company lettering on the side. "So how
is business, got a good job going on here in the mall?" Danny
asked, taking out some Kleenex to blow his nose. The guy was
now just a few feet from Danny, peering at him with squinty
eyes. He stopped suddenly. There was a few seconds of awkward
silence. Finally the strange man, with his tool bag hanging on his
shoulder replied. "No, just a small service call, that's all." With
that he went around to the side and got in the van, started it up
and left.
Danny stood there memorizing the plate number. When the van
was out of sight he took a pad out of his truck and wrote it down.
He was feeling lousy again. He reached for the Kleenex. But now
he knew this guy was up to something. In all the years in the
business one thing was certain. All contractors liked to talk to
other contractors, especially about work. You could meet a total
stranger but if he was in the same trade as you before you knew
you heard all about him. How he started out in the biz, where he
had worked before, what job he was doing now and so on. That's
how it was, guys in the same situation you were in, doing the
same stuff you were. An unwritten brotherhood so to speak. And
if you had been around long enough, you knew whether the guy
you were talking to was full of BS or not either.
And the guys who tried to BS you, they usually talked the most,
even if it was all a load. But this guy, there was something about

him and this encounter, that convinced Danny something strange was afoot.

Fred Ward squealed his tires into the parking lot and came to a rather abrupt stop by Danny's truck.

"Did you see him, is he still here? I got caught in traffic on 48, damn. And I feel like absolute shit"

"I saw him and as a matter of fact I just talked to him, if you want to call it that," Danny replied while blowing his nose yet again. "Strange guy, he is definitely up to something, I don't know what yet, but..."

His sentence cut off midway as Fred's cell phone rang. Danny heard Fred say, "Yeah I'm here with Dan Edwards, in the parking lot. He was with me at Valley View the other day when that guy was seen there.

You got what? OK, we'll be right in. Lets go Dan, Jack has a present for us."

The three of them met up by the loading dock. "Jack, this is Dan Edwards from D & E Mechanical, does a lot of good work for us over at our place." Fred introduced them.

After some small talk Jack said, "You guys sound awful, I guess I have that to look forward to now."

Danny said, "Good luck. I know it's going to be one of those type colds. It starts in your head and then after it gets bored, it goes down to your throat. It spends a few days there and finally ends up in your chest where it resides for the duration. During this time you get to buy various kinds of pretty, different colored pills all of which are very specific to where the disease is currently stationed. Some racket." They all laughed at Danny's rant. They walked back the hallway and Fred said, "So what do you have for me, Jack?"

Jack pulled the small piece of garbage out of his pocket. "Here, I saw him down by the maintenance department and followed him, he looked suspicious, always looking over his shoulder. He tossed this out during his travels, so for some reason, I fetched it out of the trash."

"Lets go check the main A/C unit down there," Danny said.

"Yeah, let's do that," agreed Fred.

They made their way down to the mechanical room and snooped around, checking for access panels and such. Danny opened the large steel door on the air handler. He pulled out his flashlight and examined the area inside, all the while the enormous fan was blasting and trying to suck the door shut. "Not much here, not that I can see anyway, can we shut this down for a few minutes? It's about ready to pull me in," Danny yelling above the noise of the fan.

Jack hit the button on the frequency drive panel that controlled the 125 horse power motor.

It slowly ramped down and finally stopped.

Danny climbed inside the massive unit. He looked down, behind the turning vanes in the ductwork, and then he saw it. A charcoal looking stain on the floor and some debris hung up under one of the vanes. A tiny piece of wire and plastic remained entangled on a return air duct sensor. He carefully removed it and wiggled his way back out. "Look familiar Freddie?" Danny exclaimed, reaching for some tissue to wipe his nose.

"Sure does Dan"came the reply, "lets head back to the maintenance office and take a closer look."

Jack hit the frequency drive controller and the big fan slowly ramped back up to speed.

They sat down at an old wooden conference table used for maintenance department meetings.

Jack pulled a magnifying glass out of a desk drawer nearby, one he used to help his failing eyesight determine model and serial numbers off the many units.

They unwrapped the bit of garbage as well. Looking closely at it Fred said, "I can't make out shit, can any of you?"

Jack said, "Well that one small thing there looks like a burned up battery for a watch or something. Hard to tell for sure. The rest of it is just plastic and of course the latex gloves. Maybe we should call the Feds in on this, this guy might be a terrorist."

They discussed the incident for awhile and looked at the evidence. Danny's cell phone rang, it was Bill.

"Hey Dan, feeling any better, I ain't. I found out some interesting stuff on our little friend." And Bill filled him on the corporate connections and info he had found out on the net.

"OK, Bill, well guess what?" And Danny told Bill about his little adventure and his meeting with the mystery man from EAQ in the parking lot.

"Weird" was all Bill could say, "Really weird, I'm going back online and see what else I can dig up, keep in touch."

Danny, Fred and Jack all discussed the new information. It was unlikely that the tie-ins with such large companies were related to terrorism, but no one expected a bunch of airliners to crash into the World Trade Center either. Still, no one had died in any malls, no evidence of airborne diseases showing up at local hospitals, no panic stricken public, nothing. In the end they thought it best to call the FBI and Jack, as head of Center City Mall, made the call. They put the evidence in a food storage bag and Jack locked it in his desk drawer.

Danny, blowing his nose yet one more time said, "Well guys, it's been fun but I am going home. I got to get some rest, the FBI will take all day getting here, I bet they get all kinds of calls for so called terrorist attacks. Since nobody is keeling over in the food court, I doubt they will see this as high priority. Let me know what you find out Freddie, OK? Nice meeting you Jack, here is a card if you ever need a good serviceman, I am available. Bye." As Danny left the mall he took out the small piece of plastic and tiny charred remains he had slipped into his pocket. He folded them into a piece of tissue and placed it on the dashboard of his truck. He had other ideas.

The phone rang in the storefront in New Jersey. "Now what?' an anxious voice answered.

"Hey, listen, some guy was snooping around my truck, I don't know what he saw but I think I need to get out of town and fast."

"Where was this at?" came the reply.

"At that last mall I hit this morning, like I told you."
"You jackass........I said to lay low, but no, you just had to do it, one more job. Damn it.
Go back to the motel and wait for my call. Can you just do that for me? No more grief, you understand. Stay there and wait."
Click.

The phone rang in an office at Chemical Imagery Group, "Hey Bob, Danny Edwards here, how you doing? I got small favor to ask, OK?
"The A/C is working fine Dan, thanks again. By the way you sound awful, I hope you are at home with that. What can I do for you?"
"Those microscopes your company developed, can they pick up anything and determine what it is?
I mean, exactly how does that work?"
Danny trying not to sniffle or sneeze during the conversation went on. "If I brought you a tiny sample of something, could you tell me what it is?"
"That depends" Bob sounding slightly hesitant now, "There is a lot we can do but we have limits, I mean there are millions of substances out there. We can narrow it down to the most common things but it would really help if we knew exactly what we were looking for. Why?"
Danny went on, "Is it Ok if I stop by? I won't take up much of your time, it's a long story."
"No problem, I have a 3 o'clock meeting that will take the rest of the day, can you get here before that?"
"I'm on my way, see you in a few, thanks."

Chapter 6

He looked more like an accountant than anything else. A tall, slender gentleman, well dressed with horn rimmed glasses who often carried a briefcase. He liked to collect antiques, expensive ones at that.

His penthouse suite in the heart of Chicago was full of them. His neighbors knew him only to be a businessman, and not much else. He was gone for days or weeks at a time and seldom mingled with his fellow condo dwellers. The doorman Roland, an older black man, knew him as Mr. Mullins and always took care of him, he tipped much better than most. Sometimes, for no real reason at all, he would put a couple hundred dollar bills in the doorman's hand and say things like, "keep your eyes on my place while I'm gone Roland, let me know if anyone shows up or any strangers are hanging around." The doorman had Mr. Mullins private cell phone number, well one of them anyway. He assumed it was because of the valuable antiques inside the plush penthouse dwelling. This day was no different than any other. The businessman was dusting off a piece of Fenton glassware when one of his cell phones rang.

"Hello," he was short and sweet and to the point, he knew too much discussion was the downfall of many men in his position. "Very well, what are the details?"

He jotted down some notes, folded the paper putting it in his briefcase.

"OK, same arrangements as before I assume, consider it done." And with that the conversation was over. He disposed of that particular cell phone in the usual place, never to be used again. The new technology of disposable cell phones made his existence more secure. He registered under fictitious names and locations that were impossible to trace. It had been a long time since he had a clandestine meeting with one of his few contacts in a dark alleyway.

He left the high rise and put a couple hundred dollar bills in Roland's hand, "Get me a taxi, and keep your eyes on my place while I'm gone, okay?"

"Yes sir Mr. Mullins, will do, thank you sir." And Rolland hailed a cab for his generous friend.

As he entered the cab he said, "O'Hare airport."

Danny pulled into the small parking lot at Chemical Imagery. As he was buzzed in the front door the receptionist said, "Problems with the A/C again?"

"No, not today," he grinned, "can you tell Bob I'm here, thanks." Danny took a seat in the tiny waiting area.

"Got a cold?" the receptionist asked.

"Yeah, how did you guess?" as Danny sneezed into some napkins he had brought along.

She just laughed and said, " I like you and all Dan, but stay over there OK, I can't afford to get sick."

Bob came around the bend and he and Danny went up to his office. Danny closed the door behind them and they both took seats across from each other.

"It's a long story," Dan explained. "Can you tell me what this is?" placing it on Bob's desk.

Bob looked cautiously at the small pile of charred debris and plastic. "What the hell you got there Dan, where did you get that?"

Danny gave Bob the quick run down of events.

"Since when did you become a private eye?" Bob joked. "If you are really concerned you should have called in the authorities. "

"We did, but in the meanwhile I was just wondering if you could speed things up here for me. I suspect that even if the feds take it serious they will keep us in the dark."

"Do you have any idea what it might be?" Bob quizzed Danny.

"Not really," came the replay.

"All I know is some mysterious contractor with ties to some large companies has been putting this in the air handlers in some of the local malls, without permission. We haven't caught him in the act but we are sure something weird is going on." Danny pressed on.

"And this is the remains of the box after you find it? It goes up in smoke and this is all that's left?" Bob asked in disbelief.

"Yes, and that plastic is from there too, part of a latex glove we think the guy wears. It was retrieved from a waste basket by one of the facility managers." Danny explained.

"OK Dan, I'm not sure what we can do here. Besides our chemical imaging scopes, we have an electron microscope that might show something. I'll get one of my technicians on it when he gets some time. Any chance this stuff is toxic? 'Bob now sounding a little apprehensive. "Maybe you guys shouldn't be messing around here. Who knows what the hell might be going on?"

"We considered that Bob," Dan went on, "But I don't see how. The contractor isn't in a chemical suit or anything. Even if he wears those cheap plastic gloves, how much protection is that? He comes and goes at will, nobody has been falling over in any stores, at least not yet." He laughed.

"OK, well you are still breathing so that's a good sign I guess," Bob joked back. "But you sound like shit, go home and get some rest, I'll let you know if we find anything."

Danny left and headed home, stopping by his shop to get the mail.

His cell phone rang, he looked at the caller ID, it was familiar but he couldn't place it. He answered hesitantly, not wanting any emergency calls right now. He already had enough excitement for one day. All he wanted now was to get home, make some soup and lay down.

"Dan Edwards here."

The voice on the other end was immediately recognized, "Hello Dan, This is Mrs. Weiser. Your guy did a great job here the other day, what a fine young man. Everything is working but….."

Here it came, Danny expecting he would have to go back.

"There is water on the floor, by the furnace, not a lot mind you, just a drip. I am going away tomorrow with one of my children. Maybe I should have it looked at, the house will be empty and I…."

Danny cut her off, "No problem, I'll have Bill stop by and have a quick peek."

"Oh, thank you so much, I feel much better being away and all." And with that she hung up.

Danny didn't want to bother Bill, being sick and all but it was probably nothing, just an overflow or loose fitting. All the lady wanted was to ease her mind. Old people were like that, nothing else to do but worry. She was a good customer though, and Bill just had to stop over and assure her the house wouldn't blow up while she was gone. Danny gave Bill a call.

"Hey, feeling any better? Can you take a quick call?"

"Yeah, I can handle it, what's up?" Bill asked.

"Old lady Weiser, some water down by the boiler. I'm sure its nothing but she is going out of town and, well, you know how that goes."

"I think the relief valve has some gunk in it," Bill said, "I noticed it the other day when I was there. I can probably get it to stop but if not it will need replaced, and that can wait till next week, right?"

"Yeah," Danny replied, "That will take some time, anyway, just go over and smack the thing, if it stops, great. If not it will at least put her mind to rest, it won't take more than 10 minutes, I'm sure."

"No problem," Bill agreeing, "I'll give her a call right now."

Danny locked up the shop and went home. He heated up some chicken soup, ate it with some bread and went up to bed even though it was early. He dozed off quickly thanks to the cold pills.

Someone crept into his room and stood over him with a long Japanese sword.

He tried to get away but he couldn't move very fast, he was in slow motion. His limbs were glued to the bed. The figure came closer. Danny yelled and his body lurched upwards, he was on the attack now, thrashing back at the ominous shadow that meant to do him harm.

"Honey, you up there?" Danny heard faintly as his eyes popped open.

He was in a cold sweat. Liz cracked the bedroom door and peered inside.

"Did I wake you, sorry." She said.

"That's OK, I have to get up now," he moaned back.

"Can I get you anything," she asked, feeling sorry for her sick hubby.

"I'm good for now, thanks. Just stay away from me, you don't want this, trust me."

Danny crawled out of bed, took a hot shower and went right back into bed. He really should have stayed home all day he realized. That's the problem with drugs he thought to himself.

They make your feel better and you go out and about. You do things instead of staying put. With that he took some more drugs and clicked on the TV in the bedroom. He heard Liz and his daughter down in the kitchen, banging some pots around and talking. They would have to eat dinner without him tonight, he was staying in bed.

He found an old war movie on one of the cable channels, one he had seen at least a dozen times. "Perfect," he said out loud. He propped himself up on some pillows so he could breathe better. Before long he had managed to nod off again, this time during the Battle of the Bulge.

As the tall slender business man hailed a cab outside the airport, he pulled out his phone. He entered the number and hit send. He sat in the backseat of the cab and told the driver to take him to the Radisson Hotel, on 9th street. He preferred that hotel when he had visited in the past. Central enough for his business and certainly large enough that average people were not noticed.

A voice on the other end of the line picked up.

"Hello." JC was laying on his bed watching a pay per view porno flick.

"I'm in town, I was told to contact you by our mutual friend at Melcher," the businessman went on. "Stay where you are, after I check in and freshen up I will be over. I need you to fill me in on some details, okay?"

JC responded in a sarcastic tone, "Whatever, I ain't going anywhere."

Then on second thought he added, " He dude, pick me up a six pack of some local beer, nothing real dark though, I'm bored out of my mind over here. Do you know where I'm staying?"

"I know, see you soon." And with that the conversation was over. JC went back to his movie, anxious to get this over with and get out of town.

Mr. Mullins checked into his room at the Radisson. He changed into some sweats, more suitable for the gym than anything else and took out his briefcase. He removed some money from it and then unpacked the small suitcase he had checked on the plane. Mullins got a sixer of beer at the hotel bar and put in the small brown bag along with some other items he had taken from his suitcase.

Then he caught another cab and directed him to the Star Lake motel on the outskirts of the city. Dusk faded to darkness as he tipped the driver just the right amount, not too much or too little to be noticed. He waited till the cab pulled away and made his way up the stairs by the pool. He knocked on the door and JC answered. "About time man, hey where is my beer?"

"Here have one. I'll buy you a nice steak too, compliments of the boss. We can discuss things over dinner and then you can get the hell out of here." JC opened a can and downed it in record time.

"Sounds good to me, I ain't making any dough sitting around this dump." JC grabbed his wallet and motel key card and they went down the stairs past the pool, drinking another brew as he walked.

"You'll have to drive, I took a cab over here," Mullins advised. "Know any good places around here?"

As they got in the minivan JC said, "I know a few, tossing the remaining beer cans on the seat. The way you are dressed we can hit one of the more casual joints I guess."

They pulled out of the parking lot and headed down the two lane road. JC asked, "So what is it you're going to do here, to clear up this mess I mean? Put a scare into those guys who are snooping around? That's what I would do." The van came to stop sign, no other traffic was around.

"Well I ain't you" Mullins mumbled and with that he reached his foot over and pushed down hard on the brake to hold it in place and quickly plunged a needle into JC's carotid artery.

He pulled the slumping body aside, pushed the gearshift into park and took control of the van, turning up the road and heading away.

"They were right, you are a stupid jackass," Mullins laughed. The antique collector drove back to JC's motel and gathered up all the belongings from the room. He packed them up and put them in the back of the van and checked out using the service provided on the appropriate TV channel. He wrapped the remains of the hypodermic syringe in the brown bag and tossed it in the bottom of the motel dumpster. He removed the special software from van's navigation system and the rest of the sealed containers. He stopped by the self storage area, entered the code and locked them inside.

He drove up a secluded road to where it overlooked a deep crevice, maybe 150 feet down an embankment.

Making sure no one was around, he got out, dumped some beer on JC, put the remaining cans on the floor of the vehicle. With JC in the drivers seat, he put it in drive and guided it over the cliff, jumping back out of the way as it started it's downward decent.

It picked up speed and then began to roll, over and over, perhaps 7 or 8 times, before crashing to a stop at the bottom of the dark hillside.

"Jackass, you really shouldn't drink and drive," he said aloud.

And with that he started jogging down the highway, off to the side of the road, with his sneakers safety flashers now blinking. Nothing like a late night run in the country he thought.

He ran the five miles back into the city and made his way to his hotel room.

He took out the notes he had made earlier, tore them up in small pieces and flushed them down the toilet. Then Mullins ordered room service and took a long hot shower. He turned in and slept like a baby.

The police report would eventually determine a self employed air conditioning contractor, working out of state, checked out of his room and was heading home. He took a few pills, drank a few beers and on a dark windy road, he failed to negotiate a turn. Toxicology reports would find alcohol and a substantial amount of a sedatives in his bloodstream. No autopsy would be preformed, no sign of foul play, no reason to waste valuable man hours looking for something that wasn't there.

Case closed.

Danny awoke to the sound of the TV. He was stuffed up and taking turns alternating between lying on his right side and then his left. When he was on his left side, his left nostril would get plugged and the same applied to his right side. It was late, everyone else was asleep in the house. He got up and took a leak. He made his way downstairs and had a snack, a peanut butter sandwich and some cookies. It made him feel better. He was sick of watching television. He stepped outside on their patio, it was cool but not cold. The night was clear, he looked up at the stars, and for a second he contemplated the meaning of his existence, as he had done so many times before out there. He had come to the conclusion there wasn't any real meaning, yet he still debated it with himself from time to time. We were just here, for a very short stay and best to make the most of it.

He started to get a chill and was heading back inside when he heard the train. His midnight train. He paused to listen as it got closer, rumbling along like an old friend he had never met. A slight wind stirred and he thought it best to get back inside, he was sick enough as it was. He took one more dose of Nyquil and crawled back into the sack.

The locomotive trailed off into the distant night air.

That night his dad paid him a visit. He was alive and well and as sharp as ever.

An ambulance and a couple police cars had gathered at the scene of the car wreck.

A tow truck was called and a coroner pulled up along side shortly after.

"Sad," the cop said to the EMT, "Maybe if he had his seatbelt on."

"Maybe if he wasn't drunk," came the reply from the paramedic.

"Yep, maybe," the officer said as he wrote down some numbers off of the crumpled van.

Chapter 7

The well dressed businessman had breakfast at a pancake house near the Radisson. It was a sunny day with just a few passing clouds. He paid his check requesting several dollars in change. Then he strolled casually down the block until he reached the pay phone on the corner near the drug store. There weren't too many pay phones left he thought to himself. Who needs them, with practically everybody owning cell phones these days they would someday become obsolete. Too bad, they were perfect for maintaining anonymity.

He picked up the receiver, deposited a few quarters and made a call.

"I'm done here," he said matter of factly. "No problems. I'll be leaving this afternoon. You can send in your crew anytime."

The man on the other end of the line responded, "I may have another job for you out there, want to stay another day until I'm sure?"

"I can stay, but I don't like surprises. You know my rate. I'll hang around here for one more day and that's it. I'll call you later tonight." And he hung up. On the way back to the hotel he window shopped some second hand stores. Sometimes you could find a valuable antique in those small, out of the way places. If you knew what to look for that is. You could get it very cheap too.

Later that day, a full size box truck pulled up to the self storage area. A young guy with sunglasses on and an earring, stopped at the gate and entered the pass code, the gate rose up. He proceeded to the selected storage area, opened it up and emptied the contents of it into his truck. He pulled out onto the road and headed east.

Bill called Danny around 8 am that morning. "What's up, chief?" he said, sounding a bit better than the day before.

Danny was still in a fog. "Not sure yet, but it's still early. How did you make out at Weisers'?"

"No biggie, I stopped the pesky drip thereby averting a major catastrophe," he laughed.

"Good job, captain courageous," Danny went on sarcastically.

"So she is happy now? I'm going to send out her bill then, unless you have to go back for something."

"Send it out," Bill replied back. "Pretty funny, she asked me to stop by and feed her dog and check the place while she is gone. Just for a couple days or so. She said I could even stay there if I wanted to. Otherwise she had to put Harry into a shelter and she didn't want to do that to the poor, old beast. She has one of them pet doors in her kitchen so the dog can go outside and do his business in some special, fenced in area. If the animal gets any fatter he is going to get stuck in it. Anyway her kid is going with her to Hilton Head. They are moving down there and she needs to close on a property."

"Wow, you had quite a long talk with her, is she planning on adopting you too?" Danny chuckled.

"I wish she would," Bill went back, "I wouldn't mind being in her will, not at all."

Danny cleared his throat,

"Maybe you could give up this repair stuff and become a professional house sitter?"

"Don't give me any ideas," Bill said, "Anyway, I'm sure she mainly trusts me because of you Dan.

Maybe she will adopt both of us."

"Yeah, maybe," Danny retorted.

"Hey guess what, I ran into our little friend yesterday, at the Center City Mall. And guess what he was doing? I even talked to him in the parking lot. He is one strange dude. We found the remains of another container in the air handler. They called in the FBI, just in case. Pretty crazy huh?"

"Very crazy," Bill went on, "that reminds me, I'm going to check and see if my bud out in Jersey got a look see at that place. I e-mailed him to swing by the address for Melcher and scope it out. So, if any calls come in, let me know, I am still feeling shitty but I can go to work."

"Right now all I got on tap is that rooftop install. We have to watch the weather, looks like a cold front moving in tomorrow and with it some pretty heavy rain. Plus it's Friday, might be better off to postpone it until next week. By then we should both be feeling better too. Matter of fact, I will call the subs when I hang up here and put it off till one day next week. It will work out better for a lot of reasons. Rest up today and tomorrow, if anything pressing comes in, you'll be the first to know."

"I will actually be the second to know, you will be the first." Bill reminded him.

"Smart ass," Danny replied, "Hey, don't forget to feed Harry, and watch out for his dearly departed master in there. He might think you are moving in on his old lady." Danny hung up and grabbed another cup of coffee.

He put on the weather channel to verify his prediction. Yep, bad storm moving in, he was glad he decided not to go ahead with that project. He called up the subs and set up a day for next week, depending on the weather of course. They could work in the cold, or in between a few light sprinkles, but not in a steady downpour. The roofers would never go for that.

Matter of fact, neither would Danny, it was just too miserable, never mind he was already sick.

He clicked down the TV dial looking for something worthwhile. He paused on one of the local channels that was showing a news report of a bad accident. A dark colored minivan missed a turn, went down a steep embankment killing the driver. Alcohol played a part in the crash. Identity withheld pending notification of the next of kin. Danny didn't give it a second thought, happens all the time.

Bill logged on and checked his mail. His old Army buddy wrote him back and attached a few pictures of the address Bill had given him. "Man," Bill said to himself, "that's Melcher Corp?" What kind of company is that he wondered, no name on the building. A small storefront in a low rent area of Jersey. What could they possibly be doing in there to make any money? He decided to try and hack into their network assuming they even had one. He knew he really shouldn't but he couldn't resist the urge.

He found a web address for them and started there. No luck, for a seemingly cheap outfit they were well protected.

He decided to just call them up and act like a salesman or something. Maybe ask them about EAQ and getting some

A/C service work done. Who knows, he would think of something.

He dialed the 800 number using his home phone. He had a private listing, meaning it was blocked to called ID and return calls. He got a standard recording asking to leave his information and they would call back. He started to leave a message, "Hi, I have an office complex in central New Jersey, I was trying to get in touch with a company called Environmental Air Quality. I know they are located somewhere in Jersey. They did some work for me last year and........."

"Hello," a raspy voice interrupted the message, "Can I help you?"

"Um, yeah," Bill now getting a bit nervous, "Like I said I was....."

"I never heard of that outfit, how did you get this number anyway? Who are you and where are you calling from?" The gruff reply came back.

Click. Bill hung up and mumbled, "Wow, was he pissed or what?"

The tall slender man was finishing up the purchase of a Yellow Cab cigar box, circa 1920. He had found it in one of the small antique stores a few blocks from his hotel. It was in mint condition and he got it well below it's value.

His phone rang, one of his disposable cell phones.

"Yes," was all he said. He listened intently and replied, "OK, I can do that, uh huh, the regular arrangement, give me a day or so to set it up. I will let you know. After that I am getting out of here, been here too long already. "

And so it was, another day and another job. The excitement began to build in his twisted mind. He enjoyed his work, the fact he got paid so well for it made it all the better.

"Is that all?" the clerk asked.

"Why no," he said, " I think I will keep shopping, what do you have in the back, any new arrivals?"

"Well we have few things in, what did you have in mind?" The clerk sensing another sale.

"Something small, I am traveling and it's hard to transport any large items," the man said looking over top his wire rim glasses.

"We do have shipping services available you know?" The clerk advised.

"Yes, I'm sure you do but something small, okay?" The man replied, obviously objecting to the implication he was an amateur and didn't know antique dealers could ship stuff right to your door.

"Well sir, we did get in some foreign currency recently. I haven't even catalogued it yet, not even sure of the price. I would have to contact the store owner," the store clerk replied now realizing his customer knew his stuff.

"Well can I at least see what you have?" came the reply.

"I suppose I could show it to you, hang on a sec," and the clerk went into the back room. He emerged with a black case and opened it up on the counter. Nothing much caught Mullin's eye except a Russian note for 5000 Roubles. It was uncirculated and unique because it was the only bank note ever issued by a military leader.

He knew this not from his expansive knowledge on coins or currency but from his fascination with Russian history.

He asked what the price was. The clerk stepped into the back room and made a call. He returned moments later.

"I can't get in touch with the owner right now, can you stop back, say tomorrow sometime?"

"Mullins hesitated, anxious to make the purchase now. He could be very impatient at times, almost demanding. But he backed off a bit.

"I will be in tomorrow morning, before lunch. After that I will be out of the area."

"I will have it priced by then, I'm very sorry sir. Please stop back in the morning, alright?"

The clerk was somewhat dismayed by the owners lack of concern with his own business. Sometimes it seemed he cared more about it than his boss. It wasn't like people were beating down the doors to get in the place.

"Very well, good day." And the gentleman picked up his cigar box and strolled out the door. He paused to check his watch. He turned around and asked the clerk, "Do you know, is that internet café still opened, the one on 3rd avenue?"

"Yes sir, I believe it is."

"Thank you, see you in the morning."

Mullins made his way to 3rd avenue and walked into the cyber café.

He got some coffee and prepaid $12 cash for one hour. Then Mullins logged onto one of the web sites using the pay for access computer.

In short order he was into a private web site forum and instructed someone to overnight him a few items. After that was taken care of, the cold blooded individual went into the web phone directory and looked up some names and addresses.

He followed that up by using Mapquest for some local driving directions. Computers and the internet sure made things much easier for everyone, especially someone in Mullins line of work.

He spent the remainder of the hour quickly surfing antique web sites and E-Bay, looking for hot deals. None could be found that day.

He returned to his hotel and informed the desk clerk to be looking out for a package for him. A special express delivery he should be getting the next morning.

He also told the clerk he would be staying an extra day or so. The clerk made a note of it, Mullins thanked him, tipped him generously of course, and went to his room.

Danny made himself a sandwich and put on the noon news. There was a story about the car wreck he had seen earlier. As he smeared some mayonaise on the bread he watched the more detailed report a little closer.

One of the shots of the wreck showed a crumpled, burnt van with police and firemen standing around.

His heart skipped a beat as he heard the reporter say, "An out of state employee of the Environmental Air Quality company was pronounced dead at the scene."

Danny heard nothing else. He sat down in amazement spreading the mayonaise over and over and over.

His phone rang. "Hello," answered Danny, not even using his typical business reply of Snyder Mechanical.

"Hey, see the news?" It was Bill.

"I sure did," Danny said.

"I am getting a little nervous about this whole thing," Bill anxiously responded.

"You and me both," Danny confirmed. "I think we may be getting in over our heads. That accident is quite a coincidence wouldn't you say?"

"It was no accident," Bill assured Dan. His military background and experience now speaking.

"Perhaps we need to back off this for now, let the authorities take over for us," Bill continued.

Not that he was afraid of the recent developments, but he was certainly aware of consequences of such an endeavor.

"I agree," Danny said. "Let concentrate on our jobs and put this little conspiracy aside for the time being.

We have enough trouble with that don't we?"

Danny nervously laughing a bit now.

"Yeah," Bill replied, "I have to go feed Harry now anyway. I can check the boiler while I am there, just for something to do."

Danny finished his lunch, switching back and forth between channels to find more information on the car wreck involving the HVAC guy who liked to put small boxes in air handlers at various malls around town.

Danny called Fred at the Valley View Mall. He gave him the info on the recent demise of their new, mysterious friend. Fred decided to pass it along to the authorities fearing they would overlook the connection.

Bill pulled up to the Weiser residence.

He went to the back door and got out his key. From the corner of his eye he though he saw something down by his truck.

He stepped back and took a good look. A dark vehicle was slowly passing by, momentarily pausing by Bill's truck.

As he walked toward the road, the car sped away.

Normally, Bill wouldn't have noticed such things but he was on a heightened state of alert, his blood ran cold.

He went back to his truck and removed the 9mm handgun he carried in the special holster under his seat.

Concealing it in his coat so the neighbors wouldn't see, he returned to the back door entrance.

His hand now gripping the automatic weapon, he slowly opened the door.

"Harry," Bill yelled, "where ya at, c'mon out."

There was an eerie stillness. Bill's heart began pounding.

The dog was nowhere to be seen. Bill slowly moved into the kitchen.

He went into the dining room and then on past the large painting of the late Mr. Weiser that hung in the front hallway. He looked up the immense, winding staircase and yelled again.

"Harry, time for chow." Nothing.

He heard a noise from the back of the house. Bill cautiously returned to the large, tile floor kitchen.

He entered the room and noticed a footprint on the tile. He crept over to the outline of the foot on the hard, ceramic tile. He put his foot on top of it, a perfect fit. How stupid he was, it was his own footprint from the damp doormat that lay right outside the back door. He laughed to himself thinking perhaps he was just being paranoid.

His hand relaxed on the gun.

At that instant, WHOOSH, Harry came reeling in through the pet entrance on the back door, sliding along the damp tile and crashing into Bill's legs. Bill's heart went right through his chest. His pulse shot up to 180 and when he finally calmed down he put the gun on the counter and started petting Harry in a rough sort of manner. He was laughing and sort of wrestling with the animal now. The kind of play that dogs enjoy, especially ones that are used to old ladies who have no interest in rough housing with them.

The stoutly, overweight bulldog had big jowls full of drool and was showing signs of old age. He was still a powerful, though compact, animal that could scare away most intruders if he felt the urge to do so.

An 80 pound dog, coming full force at you, is not to be taken lightly. Harry was as gentle as a baby but he had a protective instinct almost all dogs have.

"You scared the life out of me, you know that Harry. I didn't see ya outside there when I came in. Man, I'll tell you, I think I need a drink," Bill sat down at the table and put the gun back in his coat pocket.

"I'm glad I didn't blast you Harry, that would have been pretty hard to explain to your owner, pretty hard indeed."

Bill filled up Harry's dish, the one with his name on it, with a new can of dog food. he washed out his water bowl and filled it with fresh water as well. He played with the dog a bit more and when Harry finally settled down to eating, Bill went into the basement to double check the leaky fitting near the boiler.

The leak had almost completely stopped, nothing to worry about. As he made his way back towards the steps up to the 1st floor, he happened by a small basement window. Once used to deliver coal to the mammoth furnace, it was now replaced with glass blocks. You could still make out objects through it, though not very clearly.

In the middle was a wind out screen for fresh air intake.

His truck was in direct view from where he stood and another vehicle was slowly approaching.

Bill hurriedly wound open the screen for a better look. Once again his blood pressure was climbing.

He felt relief when he saw it was a police cruiser, no doubt stopping by to see who was parked outside the long time residents home.

Perhaps she had told them to watch her place while she was out of town.

Bill hurried up the steps and out the back door, just in time to see the officer walking up the sidewalk with his canine partner. He remembered the gun, in his pocket and hoped it didn't somehow fly out at an inopportune moment.

"I assume you are Bill?" the officer asked.

"Yes sir, that's me," Bill replied, relieved to know Mrs. Weiser had informed the police department of his dog feeding duties.

"Officer Joe Max here," He reached out his arm and the two shook hands.

"I figured it was you but still wanted to stop by and check on things," the policeman went on.

Harry came out and the two dogs started romping together.

"Harry needs some dog company every so often . So I swing by, and my partner and he go at it for a few rounds."

"I see they are well acquainted," Bill offered.

Some more small talk ensued and the two men both went their separate ways.

It would not be the last time they met in the Weiser mansion.

CHAPTER 8

Danny called Bob Baylack at the Chemical Imagery Group.
"Hey Bob, anything yet on the mysterious substance showing up at malls all over town?' Danny almost finding it funny now, for some strange reason.
"One of my guys is taking a look see right now I'll let you know as soon as we know," Bob replied, "You got me wondering about this too now, seems very odd, to say the least."
Back at the Weiser residence, Bill double checked the door locks, made sure Harry was taken care of and headed home. As he turned down the road towards the entrance ramp to the parkway, a white sedan pulled out behind him and followed at a safe distance.
Bill looked in the mirror and noticed the sedan following him, normally not that unusual but after the series of recent events, it made Bill nervous.
Bill picked up speed but suddenly deciding not to run a yellow light, slammed on the brakes. The sedan behind, trying to make the light as well, came squealing to a stop almost hitting Bill's van. Bill heard the brakes and looked in his mirror, a young kid talking on his phone waved as if to say, sorry.
"I must be getting paranoid, I have to go home and forget about this stuff," Bill thought to himself.
Meanwhile Danny went to his small home office and did some long overdue paperwork.
He took his mind off the departed EAQ technician and the burnt cardboard box by paying some bills and making out invoices. He heard his wife come home and hurry up the basement stairs, "Hey Dan," Liz yelled, "how you feeling hon?"
"A little better," Danny replied, "not great, but better, or maybe it's all the cold pills I've been taking."
"You feel like eating yet?" Liz asked.
"No, later maybe, I had a big lunch." Then he told Liz about the accident involving his mysterious mall friend.

Liz became quite concerned when Danny explained his belief that it was not an accident, but somehow related to the bizarre events of recent days.

"If you really think that Dan, then you need to call the authorities and quit snooping around. Do you really believe that?" Liz now getting on the conspiracy band wagon.

"I don't know, maybe it's the medication getting to me. Perhaps I just want it to all to be related in some devious fashion. You know, for some excitement, like in the movies" Danny tailed off and shook his head a bit. He was certainly overdoing the entire incident at this point.

For all he knew, some large company was secretly testing chemicals for air quality or something, and the guy got drunk one night and wrecked his car.

"Well," Liz said, "I'm going to the gym. Take a nap and forget all this stuff for awhile.

When I get home I'll make dinner."

Danny put stamps on the envelopes and turned to his computer to check some business records. He cleaned up some loose ends and went online to check with his web buddies, perhaps they had some info for him. Maybe they could rationalize it, Danny sure couldn't.

Danny clicked on the icon for the HVAC forum and waited for it to load up.

With his cable modem it usually came up instantly.

This time, nothing. After a bit, the error notice appeared, page not found.

Danny tried it again with the same results. He assumed their server was down either for maintenance or some technical problem. He closed it out and decided to take Liz's advice. He went up to the living room, put on the Weather Channel and laid down on the couch. In minutes he was dozing off to explanations of upcoming cold fronts and low pressure systems.

Bill pulled up to his house and backed the work van into the driveway.

As he got out and headed up the walk, a slow moving vehicle approached. The driver seemed to be looking for an address as he hesitated past each house. Bill had done that himself on many occasions looking for a customers house number.

As soon as the dark midsized car passed Bill, it sped up and pulled away.

Odd, he thought to himself. If he was looking for someone why did he leave?

Why didn't he ask Bill for directions maybe?

Oh well, after the kid in the white sedan incident, he brushed it off as more paranoia and went in the front door. It smelled like something good was cooking for dinner.

He took off his work boots and checked out the kitchen. As he lifted the lid off the big, stainless pot on top of the stove, his daughter Carly came bolting in. "Hi daddy, I helped mommy make pot roast today. Does it smell good?"

"It sure does baby doll, where is mom, anyway?" Bill asked the precocious tot.

"Right here," his soon to be wife, Robin, responded as she came up from the basement holding a laundry basket full of clean, hot, unfolded clothes. "I blew off work today and decided to get some things done around here for a change," she continued. "I have some wedding details to finalize and, oh, how is the cold?"

"Better I suppose, but Sudafed can make a lot of things seem better," Bill replied as he backed away trying not to spread his infectious disease.

"I'm going to hit the shower, give me the clothes, I'll fold them when I am done up there."

"I got it under control hon," she said. "Take your shower and I'll serve you a nice, hot meal for a change."

With them both working dinners were often hit and miss. Bill cooked more than Robin did since he usually got home first.

As Bill walked by the front door and headed up to the bathroom he noticed the dark midsized car. It slowly went past his house again and sped away down the street in similar fashion.

He didn't like that, not a second time. He would keep his eyes peeled for the rest of the evening, his 9mm not far away.

After a tremendous feast fit for a king, Bill was to relax the rest of the night in his large, overstuffed recliner, watching TV. He often spent this time with his daughter but feared giving her his awful cold.

It worked out well that she was picked up by the parent of her closest friend, Molly, for a sleepover that night anyway.

Robin tapped Bill on the shoulder around 10 pm. "Why don't you just go up to bed, it will be more comfortable than sleeping there," she surmised.

He awoke with a jolt and peered out the window.

"What are you looking for?" Robin asked.

"Nothing,….. I dunno, nothing really. I'm okay here for awhile. Go up to bed if you want, I'll be up in a sec." And Bill shut off the TV as well as the light. Robin went up to the bedroom. Bill saw headlights coming up the road, he perked up and focused his sleepy eyes on the approaching beams of light.

Danny had also grown weary from the war raging on in his body between good and evil.

A virus has no real cure, only time and the bodies natural defenses will eradicate it from your system.

Between that battle and the effects of Sudafed Severe Cold pills, Danny had slept through the evening. Liz had let him sleep too, it was the best thing for him. She had made herself some cereal and read her book in bed until she too faded off to dreamland.

Danny's cell phone was vibrating on the coffee table. He slowly came to realize that fact and grabbed it as the Local On The 8's went over the current and upcoming forecast.

He turned off the television and answered in a groggy voice, "Hello."

"Dan, its Bill. I'm sorry to bother you, hope you weren't sleeping man. But I'm getting worried about this whole thing. The dead EAQ guy, the burnt box's, I mean……."

Danny cut him off. "Yeah, well I agree but how about we worry about it tomorrow. This cold is still kicking my ass."

"Well, OK, but there is this car that seems to be cruising around my house a lot. I saw it twice earlier and just now it came by again. It's starting to freak me out, I even got the 9 handy."

"The same car, you sure it's the same car?" Danny asked back.

"Well, it's dark out now but I would have to say, yes. Yes, I'm sure, it's the same one, went real slow and then took off after it passed my house. It just went by again and I was watching it with the lights out. It parked up the road and just sat there. Whoever was in it, turned off the headlights and is just sitting there. I'm sure it isn't just a coincidence, it can't be. What with all that went on the last couple days, something is up. I can feel it."

"Call the police," Danny commanded. "Tell them there is a suspicious vehicle in the neighborhood. Could be a burglar, who knows. You don't have to go into the crazy story about the dead guy and the malls and all that. Just tell them you think someone is casing your house"

"Yeah, I suppose I should. It can't hurt. I'll call you back in a few, you gonna be up?" Bill asked his boss.

"Well I doubt I can sleep now, after all this ruckus. Plus I slept all afternoon." And Danny shut off the lights in his house and looked out the window, wondering if they were both delusional or both in danger.......

Chapter 9

Bill dialed 911. "Hello, emergency services, can we help you?" A women's voice answered.

Bill paused and then responded, "Umm, never mind, everything is OK, sorry."

The lady replied, "Are you sure, you are not in danger are you?"

"No, I'm fine, I thought there was someone watching my house but it's probably nothing." Bill said.

"OK then, but if you think anything is wrong, let us know. That's why we are here." She answered back.

"Will do, sorry." And with that Bill hung up and continued his vigil watching out his window for the mysterious dark coupe.

As he began to doze off, the phone rang and startled him right out of his Lazy Boy.

"Well, did you call them?" Danny asked.

"You scared the hell out of me Dan" Bill scolded him.

After Bill regained his composure, he continued.

"Yes, I mean no, I called, but then changed my mind. There isn't anyone out there now anyway so why bother.

If I see anything suspicious I'll call the police, for sure."

"10-4" replied Danny, "If you need anything let me know, I'm up watching Dirty Harry and his 44 magnum, the most powerful handgun in the world, it can blow your head clean off."

"One of my favorite Clint Eastwood lines too," Bill laughed back, "night Dan."

Danny relaxed and concentrated on the movie, he put the days events out of his head.

His eyes became heavy, and he turned the volume down a bit. He awoke to gunshots, just in time to see Harry Callahan blast the perp into oblivion.

He shut off the TV, went up to bed and as he laid down in the spare bedroom he heard his train come rumbling down the tracks. It was late, he thought.

As his mind took over while his body became limp, he ended up in the middle of a family party. It was at the old house Danny grew up in, even his brothers, whom he hadn't seen in years, were there. They looked good, as though time had stood still for all of them.

The basketball hoop was rusty and the ball needed air, but the Edwards brothers were ageless.

Memories and images, hidden away in a miniscule speck of gray matter were brought back, larger than life itself.

Bill heard a vehicle approach up the street. He peered out hoping it was nothing but saw the dark car stop up the road once again. He called 911 and this time he asked for a patrol car to come by. As he waited for the police, the car once again, as though playing some sort of cat and mouse game, drove off.

The officer came to the door and Bill answered.

"I don't know what's going on, but a dark car keeps driving by here. It stops up the road and then leaves a short time later. No one gets out of the car. It's freaking me out." Bill explained leaving out any fears he had about the EAQ guy and the cardboard box.

"Well sir, " the policeman replied, "I will stay around the neighborhood here for a time, if that makes you feel any better. If the automobile returns we'll see what's going on. He may be casing a house or something, who knows."

"Thanks," Bill said, "I really appreciate it."

The police officer returned to his squad car and pulled it back into a side street and shut off his lights.

A half an hour passed and nothing. Right about that time someone broke into a local drug store and set off a silent alarm. The cop had to respond in kind. As he turned on his flashing lights and squealed his tires out of the alley, Bill made a decision. He woke up his future wife and said "C'mon, lets get out of here."

"What's going on" Robin asked in a dazed state of confusion.

"It has to do with that whole incident at the malls, and the dead guy."

"Bill, your getting carried away, lets go back to bed."

But Bill insisted, he just had a bad feeling about it.

"I have the keys to the Weiser house," Bill said, "We can go there for the night until I figure out what's going on.

Hurry up, grab a few things and lets go."

Robin gave up arguing, her daughter was out for the night and she had never seen Bill this worked up before.

So they headed out to the Weiser home in Bill's work van. Bill decided that if the police saw his work truck at the empty house they would know who it was, based on the last encounter with them there.

As they pulled into the driveway at the Weisers, a dark vehicle followed several blocks behind, and parked on an empty side street.

The rain storm was accompanied by strong winds. The venetian blinds blew wildly while the water coming in the side window above the bed in the guest room at the Weiser home, finally woke Bill up. He could hear Harry barking. It was 5 a.m. The house was dark but the bolt of lightening that seemed to hit right outside lit up the room for just an instant.

In that moment Bill saw the shadow of a man pass by the upstairs hallway.

His mind and heart raced, he leapt from the overstuffed bed. The dark figure was once again lit up by lightning, now moving towards Bill. A gunshot rang out. Bill felt it graze his arm as he hit wildly at his attacker.

Both men tumbled to the ground, their limbs locked. They wrestled out the door and crashed down the stairs. Robin screamed at the top of her lungs. Harry's bark became frantic. More lightning lit up the huge mansion. Robin screamed in absolute terror once again and more barking from the English Bulldog named after his deceased owner.

As they hit the landing at the bottom of the huge staircase, they separated. Bill was dazed and his left arm was in pain.

The intruder was getting up and reaching for the gun which lay under the mural of the late Mr. Weiser.

At that precise moment Harry barreled across the room and he hit the assassin like a ton of bricks. His mouth was entrenched on his leg as he drove him back against the wall. The painting came down on top of them. It appeared as if the spirit of Mr. Weiser was still indeed an inhabitant of his former estate, protecting his property and those who did right by him.

Bill yelled for Robin to get out and she hurried out the back hall and down the stairs by the servants quarters.

Mullins had the gun and blindly fired off a few shots. That freed him from the dog who took cover under a couch.

Bill hobbled out of the living room and down the dark stairs into the cellar. He made his way to the fuse panel and killed the main switch. The boiler was smoking hot and he snuck back behind it and crouched down near the circulating pump. The contract killer slowly eased his way down the stairs after Bill. His shadow grew closer to the furnace. It was dark save for the occasional lightning which momentarily lit up the room.

The floor was concrete and no sounds came from the footsteps which edged their way around the old, somewhat cluttered cellar. Mullins approached the large boiler and made his way around the back, the gun held tightly in his hand.

Bill had no choice, he couldn't run at this point. He lunged at the killer and grabbed the hand with the gun in it, more shots were fired. They were embraced back against the hot furnace. Mullins put his left hand on Bill's throat and squeezed. Bills left arm was broken and he winced in pain as he tried to free the death grip from the experienced attacker. Bill saw the relief valve right near Mullins face, the one that had been leaking.

He grabbed the arm on top of the valve and popped it up causing hot water and steam to blast into Mullins face.

The killer yelled in pain and released his grip, Bill backed away and tripped over some cast iron piping attached to the furnace.

Mullins let go of the gun and bolted from the room, his hands on his blistered face.

He made his was back to the car and disappeared from sight.

A police siren wailed in the distance, growing closer by the second. Bill made his way back upstairs and out onto the lawn where Robin was hiding behind some overgrown shrubs. They embraced and fell back on an

Adirondack chair as the lights from the police car could be seen coming up the street.

The rain had stopped almost as abruptly as it had began.

Harry appeared from the darkness and began licking Bill's left hand,which hung down from his side.

"Good old boy," Bill said as he petted the dog with his good arm, "I owe you one buddy."

Mullins drove down the dark road leaving his lights off until he got far enough away to remain incognito.

He was so upset with himself it overcame the pain of the burn to his face.

"How could I have messed that up?" He said out loud. In all his years he had never botched a job like that.

"I'm getting too old for this," he admitted under his breath.

"I knew better than to take on that second contract, I should have left town when I had planned. It's their fault, damn it."

But he knew in his heart it was his own stupid mistake. He returned to the hotel as the sun tried to make it's way through the rain clouds.

The lobby was empty except for a clerk who remained in the back office area. Mullins covered his face and took the elevator up to his floor. When he got in his room he surveyed the damage to his face. It was beginning to blister. He took some pain pills, which he always brought along when he traveled, and held cool, wet towels on his face as he lay down on the bed.

"Damn it" he muttered one more time.

Bill asked Robin to go get his cell phone, he needed to call Danny.

What if the assassin was on his way over there now?

Bills broken arm began to swell and turn blue.

Officer Joe Max pulled his cruiser up the drive and came to an abrupt halt. He emerged from the car with his canine in tow and his hand on his revolver. Harry rumbled his way across the grass to greet them.

"What in the world is going on here?" Officer Max asked in disbelief. "Is everyone alright?"

As Robin came running out of the house with the cell phone, Joe Max gripped his gun and shone his heavy duty flashlight upon her. "Who the hell are you? What is going on?"

Bill gave the policeman the Cliff notes version of the entire fiasco.

Then he asked, "I have to make a call to my boss, he may be in danger too. I have to get to the hospital, I think I broke my arm. Can I explain all this later?" He winced in pain and tried to press his arm to his body so it wouldn't move.

"Want an ambulance?" the officer asked.

"No, she can take me," Bill replied nodding towards Robin.

Another police siren was heard approaching in the distance. As it grew near Bill dialed Danny's number. Officer Joe Max asked.

"Are you sure no one else is in the house?"

"I saw someone run out, and then heard his car leave from up there in that alley," Robin responded. "Unless he had help in there, the house is empty."

The officer put out an APB on the vehicle and requested local hospitals to be on the lookout for someone with a bad burn on his face.

Then the policeman let his dog loose in the house, he gave a command which instructed the large German Shepherd to, "search and destroy" should he encounter anyone. When his back up arrived they entered the home with guns drawn.

Chapter 10

As Robin drove Bill to the hospital he called Danny.

No one picked up, it was early he thought. He left a message briefly describing his ordeal.

Danny would know what it was about.

The police came out of the house with the dogs. By that time a detective had arrived and was brought up to date by officer Max. The whole incident seemed peculiar to the policemen, they would need to talk to Bill as well as Danny and as soon as possible.

Danny stumbled down the stairs, groggy from the cold pills he had been taking.

He grabbed a cup of coffee and walked into his home office. It was more like a den area he used for work as well as pleasure.

His phone machine was blinking with one new message. He hit the play button.

"You have one new message from Bill Strathmore." The machine told him in a robot sounding voice, also giving him the date and time of the call.

As Danny listened to it his eyes finally opened all the way.

"What the hell!" He thought to himself out loud.

He returned the call but Bill was already in the emergency room and unable to answer.

Liz came down getting ready to head off to work and saw Danny's demeanor.

"What's wrong hon?" she asked.

"I don't know for sure but we may not be safe here anymore." Danny replied.

Liz sat down in amazement. She sipped her morning tea and listened to the developments as Danny understood them.

The phone rang with an alarming blare. They both jumped out of their skin as the silence was broken by the obtrusive noise.

"Hello," Danny answered not even using his typical business response of Edwards mechanical.

"Mr. Edwards?" An unfamiliar voice asked.

"This is he," Bill reluctantly responded.

"This is detective Conner, we need to talk to you ASAP concerning the incident at the Weiser residence last night. Would it be possible for you to come downtown and answer some questions for us?"

The detective was calm yet demanding.

"Your man, Bill Strathmore, was involved in a break in and some sort of assault. Have you talked to him yet?" the detective went on.

"He left me a message on my machine, must have been early this morning. I just got it and tried to reach him," Danny went on.

"But he didn't pick up. He said he was on the way to the hospital, I know you can't use your cell phone in the emergency rooms, so...."

"What did he say?" the detective's voice cutting him off in mid sentence.

Danny paused and became somewhat paranoid.

"Who is this again?" Danny asked, now wondering what was real and what wasn't.

"It's detective Conner, like I said, we need some information. Bill is unavailable at the moment. It won't take long, how about we meet for coffee at the Hillcrest diner, you know where that is? Say in 20 minutes, I'll buy. Either that or we can haul you in and do this downtown under less favorable conditions." The police investigator now sounding a bit agitated.

"Oh, okay, make it 45 minutes, I just woke up. I'll be there." Danny responded. He tried to reach Bill again but his voicemail picked up the call. And with that he got dressed as a million thoughts raced through his head.

Mullins clicked his disposable cell phone shut. He got a scarf for his face, gathered up his belongings including a handgun and a long thin knife from his briefcase and made his way down the back stairs of the hotel.

Before he left, he used the room TV to check out and even wiped off the doorknobs and dressers with a hotel wash cloth. It was time for him to wrap this up and get out of town.

The ER doctor set Bills arm in a plaster cast and secured it from moving with a tight sling apparatus.

"Pretty nasty break there." he said as he finished.

"How did you get it?"

Bill paused for a few seconds. "It's too long to go into right now I'm afraid. You got anything for pain doc, it's really starting to hurt. Between that and this cold I have, I would just like to go to sleep."

"I'll give you a script for something." The young doctor replied. "Take it easy for awhile, try not to use it at all. In a month it should be a lot better, maybe in six weeks or so the cast can come off." And the physician handed Bill a hastily written prescription for a pain killer and a sleep aid.

"Go easy on these things," the doctor said, "only take them as needed. Any problems develop in the meantime, get back in here."

Danny laced up his sneakers and slurped on his coffee. He asked Liz if she could call off work and take their daughter to visit her mom for a day or so.

"Is it that serious Dan?" she asked.

"I'm not sure, but I think it would be a good idea for you guys to stay out of sight for awhile" Danny finding it hard to believe what he was saying.

Liz called the school's number for reporting off and left the information. She stuck her head in the bedroom and yelled to her daughter to get up. As she packed a few things she dialed her mother's phone. It was early but she knew her mom would be already up.

As she began explaining her upcoming visit, Danny rousted his daughter and briefly described the situation, without going into any details.

As they pulled out of the driveway, Danny locked the door and followed them at a distance until they turned onto the highway. He then proceeded to the Crestview Diner. He was a few minutes late but he had to make sure his family was safe before his meeting with the detective.

Bob Baylack's head lab tech walked into his office.
"You know that small, burnt box you wanted us to analyze?" He asked Bob. "The one from the mall?"
"Yeah," Bob answered back, "did you come up with anything?"
"I had to consult with a friend of mine at the CDC in Atlanta but we are pretty sure we found something, something very unusual."

As Danny pulled into the diner, his cell phone rang.
"Dan" the familiar voice asked, "Bob here, I have some information you might be interested in. Can you swing by this morning?"
"Sure thing, Bob. I'll be by after my meeting with the police. I'll explain later, thanks, gotta go."
As Bob was asking him about the meeting with the policeman, his phone call disconnected.

As Bill left the ER a policeman was waiting for him in the lobby.
"Bill Strathmore?" He asked.
"That's me" he responded .
"Can you please come with me? We need to get some information from you. It won't take long. I can ride you to the station." The young cop replied.
Robin said she was going to go pick up their daughter from her sleepover and would meet Bill later at home.
"Don't go home right now," Bill exclaimed, "can you stay with your sister for the time being?"
And with that they hugged and Robin made a call to her only sibling on her cell phone.

In the patrol car, Bill asked if he could make a call, to his boss.
"I don't see why not." The policeman replied.

Danny flipped open his phone as he pulled into the parking lot of the diner.

"Hey chief, did you get my message? Wow, what a night, I am just leaving the hospital now, going to the station for some questioning." Bill went on without even taking a breath. "It's really getting crazy, none of us are safe, we need to……"

Danny cut him off, "Yeah, I know, I am going to meet a detective myself, right now, at the Crestview Diner. He wants to know what happened last night with you and that whole mess at the Weiser's house. I sent Liz to her moms."

"I told Robin to go to her sisters." Bill retorted back.

"Alright Bill, well I have to go, I am already late. Some Detective named Conner is probably pacing in the diner, all ready to send out an APB on me or something." Danny trying to break the tension with a little humor now.

"We can meet up later, at Chemical Imagery, Bob has some info on that little device we found. I'll call you when I am done."

"Sure thing Dan, maybe we can get to the bottom of it. I have had about enough of this nonsense."

As Bill put his phone in his belt holder he mentioned to the officer, "Hey if you get an APB from Detective Conner, looking for a Mr. Dan Edwards, I know where he is." Slightly grinning to himself.

"Detective Conner?" the cop asked back. "He retired 3 years ago. Took an early out, had some back problems. A whole bunch of them went on a golden handshake type deal. They got a bonus plus guaranteed health care till they hit 65. That's how I got hired, they made room for more of us uniformed boys and moved some other guys up the ladder."

Bill paused and thought for a second.

"You sure about Conner being gone? He doesn't have any relatives there or someone else with the same name?"

"I'm sure," the cop replied back. "It isn't that big of a department, we all know each other. There was no other Conner except Tom Conner, who retired like I said. Why? "

Bill frantically called Danny back on his cell. All he got was his voicemail.

"How far are we from the Crestview Diner?" Bill asked. "It's right up the road here, isn't it?"

"I am to take you directly downtown.," the officer responded back in no uncertain terms.

"Look," Bill exclaimed. "I was almost killed last night. See this cast on my arm? It's a long story. All I can tell you is right now my boss may be in danger. He is suppose to be meeting some detective Conner, who you said left the force some time ago. So something is going on, it can't hurt to swing by and check it out can it?"

The patrol car suddenly took a hard right turn. As the tires squealed the red light went on and the siren blared.

"Happy now?" the policeman asked, with a slight smile on his face.

He joined the force looking for some excitement anyway, who knows, this might turn out to be pretty good.

Chapter 11

Danny walked in the front door of the restaurant and took a seat in a booth by the window.

He looked around the small establishment and didn't see anyone that looked like a detective, nor did he notice anyone trying to find him.

"What will it be dear?" An older bleach blond waitress wearing entirely too much makeup asked him.

"Coffee please." Danny responded back, still perusing the diner for officer Conner.

"Looking for someone?" she inquired.

"Well, yes, I am suppose to meet a detective. Do you know an officer Conner by any chance?"

"Tom Conner?" she replied back.

"I don't know his first name," Danny said back, now thinking how odd this whole situation was.

Why would a policemen ask to meet him here?

"I know a Tom Conner," the waitress went on, "He was a county detective, I used to date his brother. Anyway, Tom retired a few years back. You sure about the name?"

"Right now I'm not sure about anything." Danny admitted.

Mullins waited outside in a stolen car he had acquired easily from the hotel parking garage. When he saw Danny go in, he pulled his vehicle over by Danny's truck.
He got out and opened the hood, looking around inside as if something was wrong with the engine.
Soon Dan would eventually give up on the fake meeting, come back out and inquire as to what the problem was.
It would be then that Mullins would make his move. The knife would be quieter but the gun would be the back up if necessary.
Then he would ditch the hot ride, return to the hotel, get his rental car and get out of town.
It was much riskier than most of his jobs, but things had gone wrong. He was determined to get these guys now and his usual careful planning and cunning had gone by the wayside..

"Well, so much for Conner" Dan said out loud as he grabbed the check off the older, Formica table top.
"He knows how to reach me, if he even exists." Danny muttered.
"What?" The hostess said as she rang him up.
"Nothing, it's a long story, too long." Danny pushed open the glass door and walked towards his truck.
He saw the stranger bent over the open hood of the car, which was parked right next to Dan's truck.

At that moment a police siren wailing in the distance seemed to be coming rapidly closer.
"Now what?" Danny thought.

He turned in the direction of the noise just in time to see the patrol car swing around the two lane blacktop and head his way.
He stared in amazement as it came to a stop right in front of him.
He was even more shocked when Bill Strathmore jumped out of the front passenger door.
"Hey man, you OK?" Bill quizzed him in a panic ridden tone.
"I don't know, am I? Danny asked now looking at the young policeman also getting out and heading his way.

Bill and the cop told Danny about detective Conner being off the
police force.
"Maybe you both better come downtown with me," The
uniformed officer explained.
"The FBI is involved now, my captain just radioed me to get
down there, ASAP."
"No problem, but I'll follow you in my truck if ya don't mind,
don't want to leave it here." Danny consenting to the request.
Danny turned, and headed towards his Chevy work van taking
the keys out of his pocket as he got near it.
The stranger was gone.
Danny pulled his truck up behind the patrol car and lightly
touched his horn as if to say, ready when you are.
They both drove out of the decaying parking lot and headed
down the highway towards the county police station.
Mullins turned up a dirt road until it became impossible to go any
further on the forgotten path. He parked behind some woods, out
of sight from the main road. He got out his maps and driving
directions he had downloaded off Mapquest the day before. The
frustrated contract killer tuned in a radio channel playing
classical music and pondered his next move.

"Look guys, I need to know what is going on. I need to know
right now, all of it." The FBI inspector asked Dan and Bill as they
sat in old wooden chairs in the musty police station.
The police detective also jumped in, "You know, one of you
could be dead right now. Matter of fact, you could both be dead.
Lets have it."
At that moment Fred Ward, the maintenance manager from the
Valley View Mall was brought in to the room.
The FBI detective said, "Good, now we are all here."

"We need to get Bob Baylack here too. " Danny said, "he ran
some tests for me on the contents of one of those box devices.

He runs Chemical Imagery and has access to some high tech microscopes and such. He called me this morning and said they had some info on it. I guess the CDC got involved too."

Danny now thinking he stepped over the line with his little bit of detective work.

"What?" both the police detective and FBI inspector said simultaneously.

"It's a long story, like I told the hostess at the Crestview Diner, a very long story." Danny confessed.

"The hostess at the Crestview Diner?" The inspector quizzed in a startled tone, "Is she involved too, do we need to get her in here as well?"

"Let me start at the beginning," Danny remarked. "Let's slow down here and figure this out. Fred already called you guys in so you knew something was going on." Looking towards the FBI man.

And with that they all put the story together each taking turn filling in the details as they knew them.

The phone rang at Chemical Imagery, Bob was summoned to the phone. A short time later both he and his head lab tech waited in the lobby.

As a police cruiser pulled up in front of Chemical Imagery Group, they both went out.

In short order they were involved in the discussion between Dan, Bill, Fred, an FBI inspector, a lead police detective, a stenographer and a young, uniformed policeman.

"It's what?" The young policeman blurted out, as the detective and inspector now both glared at him for taking over the conversation.

"It's some type of ultra resistant virus, a cold and flu type. Different from anything ever seen at the CDC." The lab tech explained. "It is highly contagious, extremely virulent, easily transmitted by air or contact and resistant to most common environments that would normally kill it. Anyone coming in contact with it would surely come down with a nasty cold with possible flu like symptoms."

At that moment, Bill sneezed violently. He and Danny both just looked at each other.

"But why?" the detective asked in amazement.

Bill piped in suddenly realizing the connection.

"Think about it. A large pharmaceutical corporation, who makes millions, no, billions of dollars off cold remedies, needs to be assured their products will fly off the shelves.

They acquire smaller companies to not only cover their tracks but assist in the elaborate scheme. Many of the smaller players didn't even know about it. So you have Rycon-X as the head honcho and Melcher Co. as the cover for them."

Danny jumped in. "EAQ as the henchmen and stores like Lydia's as unknowing participants, pawns in the plan so to speak."

"All this to sell cold pills?" the FBI inspector asked out loud, in a tone realizing the validity of the accusations just presented.

"It's a billion dollar a year industry," the police detective reiterated. "I'm not usually one for crazy conspiracy theories but …."

"Nothing would surprise me these days, especially with that much money involved." Danny piped in "And with money comes power, and in time power corrupts almost everyone who has it. They are never satisfied, it is sickness, like drugs or gambling and just as bad if not worse."

The room became suddenly quiet as Danny halted his rant. The young policeman spoke up after what seemed an eternity. "So now what, who do we arrest, how can we prove it?"

The FBI inspector picked up the phone, he made a call to the head office.

"Yes, you heard me," he said, "contact the attorney general of the United States if need be. We need to get on this with the biggest guns we can muster, and fast."

The FBI took control of the investigation.

Meanwhile, Dan, Bill and the rest gave statements and were allowed to go home.

"We will give you police protection if you want it, at least for 48 hours, until we can get some answers." The detective offered.

"I think I'm alright on my own," Danny said. "My family is out of town for now, I can take care of myself."

"Yeah, me too," Bill agreed. "I won't know who is watching me, the good guys or the bad guys, it will just make me more nervous.'

"Well, it's up to you," and the detective gave them each a card with his private cell phone number on it.

"Call me if anything comes up. I always answer that line, day or night."

"Thanks" they both said in unison.

"Well, I have some work to do at the office, you can take your one good arm home and rest. C'mon, I'll give you a ride." Danny opening up the passenger side door of his truck for Bill. "Or, since our better halves are out of town, you can stay with me for a few days. We might be better off if we kept an eye on each other."

"Sounds good to me," Bill replied back. "I'm out of food anyhow. But I am okay, I'll hang with you at the office for awhile. Can we swing by the drugstore so I can get this scrip filled, my arm is starting to throb.

The doc gave me a shot of something but it is starting to wear off."

'You hungry?" Dan asked.

"I can eat, hell, I can always eat" Bill laughed.

"We'll stop for something, it's time for lunch. Maybe go back to that Crestview Diner, just for kicks."

Danny turned on to the highway and headed back the way they had come. As they pulled into the parking lot of the diner, Danny peered around, still wondering why he had been summoned there by someone. Someone no doubt involved in the whole fiasco.

An unmarked car followed their every move. The police detective wasn't taking any chances and had put the young patrolman on their tail.

Dan wrapped up his paperwork as Bill slept on the old, beat up couch in the back of the shop.
He put off his service calls, he couldn't concentrate on work anyway.
Maybe tomorrow he would be ready. He spent some time lining up the bigger rooftop installation the following week, organizing a job like that well in advance was key to its success.
Dan sat back in the reclining, desk chair and closed his eyes. In no time he was dozing off as well.
He dreamt about being chased, a large train was coming at him, he was stuck on some railroad tracks and could only move in slow motion. The harder he tried, the slower he went, the locomotive came closer and closer.

"Hey, lets go" Bill shook Dan out of his dream state with a jump. "You done here?" he asked.
"Oh, yeah, I am ready to go" and Danny and Bill locked up the shop and went back to Dan's house. Along the way they went by Bill's and he got a few things. They both called their significant others and gave them an update.
"I'm really worried about you Dan." Liz exclaimed. "I would feel better being home right now."
"Give me a couple days, OK hon? Dan asked. "I can't be fretting over you guys right now, I feel much better knowing you are safe and out of the way of whatever the hell is going on here."

The rest of the day was uneventful, the guys played a few games of Backgammon, made some soup and ham sandwich's for dinner and put on ESPN to watch a college football game. Every car that came up the road was scrutinized by one of them, they all passed on by just like any other day.

Around 10 pm Dan said, "Hey, I'm going to bed, the spare room is all yours. How's the arm?"
"It's sore but not too bad, it was just a slight crack, that's what the x-ray showed. So, I'll live."
 Bill replied.
The young policeman sitting in his vehicle a few blocks away, radioed his boss. "Nothing going on here, want me to stay?"
"Give it one more hour, than pack it in." The call came back.
" 10-4" Was the response.
Bills arm was beginning to ache again, it was after eleven and he got up to take another pain pill.
As he climbed back in bed he heard another car approach. He was too tired to get back up and check it out.
But when the engine quit out in front of the house, he realized someone had stopped there.
He jumped back out of bed and pulled the drapes ever so slightly.
 A dark sedan was parked a few houses up on an otherwise vacant street.
Bill sat there just watching it for five minutes or so, he decided he would wake Dan up, they would call the detective if anything suspicious went on.
The sedan started its engine and left, the young policeman was on his way home.
Bill shook it off and went back to bed, he was getting paranoid, he had his 9mm on the night stand, just in case.

A cold front was moving in. On cool, crisp nights, sounds traveled more easily through the night air.
Some snow flurries whipped up but didn't accumulate.
Danny couldn't sleep, he too had heard the car out front but also dismissed it as nothing.
Maybe the sound of his train would help him fall asleep, where was it?
It was still early yet he figured.

A dog barked in the distance. The bark became more aggressive like dogs do when someone invades their territory, then it stopped.
Danny's eyes closed.

Several minutes later the sound of breaking glass came from somewhere in the basement of Danny's house.
Bill and Dan literally flew out of bed, they frantically met in the hallway, Bill clutching the Smith and Wesson handgun ever so tightly in his good hand.
"Call the Detective" Bill whispered in a rather loud voice.
"No time for that," Danny responded. "Shhh," he continued. "We need to calm down and think."
" I think we need to get the hell out of here." Bill said.
"Yeah, lets go,"and they crept quietly down the dimly lit hallway towards some back stairs that led to the kitchen. "We can go out through the garage and get my truck in the driveway." Danny surmised in a barely audible tone.
"We'll call the detective and try to lose this joker."
"You sure he will follow us?" Bill asked.
"I would say at this point, yes. I hope that's loaded" Dan said eyeing the 9 that Bill was holding.
"Most definitely," Bill assured him, "I have the 15 shot clip in here."
"Good, we may need it." And Danny pointed down the dark stairs toward the garage door, "that way."
They reached the bottom of the stairs and slowly moved across the floor. Danny grabbed a hoodie and an older work jacket hanging by the door, he handed one to Bill who was only in some sweats and a tee shirt. Bill brushed against a pot handle sticking out from the cook top as he put on the coat.
It crashed to the floor braking the silence with a bang.
Shots rang out from the other end of the house. They bolted into the garage and out the side door by the end of the driveway.
Danny grabbed the truck keys off a hook in his garage as he raced by.

He unlocked the door and scooted in, reaching over and unlocking the passenger side for Bill.

More shots were fired and one pierced the back panel of the van. "Damn, that was close" Dan screeched.

The engine cranked over and Danny floored it as they peeled out of the driveway. The back window shattered with yet another bullet.

"Go, man, go" Bill yelled. And they headed out on the quiet street like gangbusters.

Bill swung back his weapon to return fire but saw nothing.

"I'm freezing my ass off" Danny said as he finally took a moment to put on the hooded sweatshirt.

"Yeah, it sure is cold out here all of a sudden," Bill agreed. "And the snow is picking up quite a bit too."

"Now what, I left my cell phone in the room. And the card from the detective is in my other pants pocket." Danny remarked.

"Let go the police station, or stop at a pay phone and dial 911" Bill suggested.

"Not sure we have time for that right now" Danny replied as he nodded towards the rear view mirror at some headlights following them in the distance.

"Just pull over and let's have it out with this guy already" Bill said in stern voice, "he broke my arm, tried to kill me and is generally making my life miserable."

"What if he ain't alone?" Danny replied back, "or what if he has an automatic weapon or some crazy shit like that?"

In the distance Danny heard his train approaching.

He thought out loud for a second. "If I can get up to Frey road and over the tracks, at the crossing gate right near the bridge, he will have to wait for the train to pass."

He knew how long that would take. It would be plenty of time for them to get away.

"Go for it" Bill egged him on.

Danny swung a hard left and headed up the steep hill.

The train whistle got louder and louder. Then the shorter bursts began, signaling it was near the crossing gate.

Danny saw the gate ahead and the train's single, bright beam moving along the hillside towards them.

The snow was coming down harder, visibility worsened.

Danny swerved to the right and bounced his front right wheel off a large rock on the side of the road.. Bang, the tire popped, he lost control and spun around coming to a stop, the back of his truck sitting on the tracks. Ding, ding, ding, the alarm bell sounded and red lights on the gate lit up. The large gates arm moved downward, brushing against the front of the truck, pinning them in between the tracks and the gate.

The lights following them in the distance came up the hill at a high rate of speed.

"Put it in reverse and get out of here!" Bill yelled.

"I'm trying," Danny yelled back.

The train was coming down the tracks right at them, dead on. The car was flying towards them from the road.

Danny somehow ground the gear in reverse. He slammed the pedal to the floor, the back wheels screeched and rubber began burning. The flat tire sheared off completely and the bare wheel sparked along the road.

All he could see were lights, from the side and the front, almost on top of him.

The van jolted backwards off the tracks and smashed through the other gate. It kept going for several yards until it rolled, out of control, into a ditch. It came to a sudden halt at a 15 degree angle. Smoke came out from under the hood.

Mullins kept coming, his blistered face swelling up causing his eyes to squint.

He hit the closed gate and slammed on through, his gun already aiming out the window.

The diesel locomotive hit him squarely. The tremendous force caused his car to explode instantaneously into a huge ball of fire.

"Did you see that?" Bill asked Dan in amazement.

For once in his life, Danny was speechless.

The train dragged the wreckage for well over a half mile.
There wasn't much left by the time the police arrived, just a large,
burnt piece of twisted metal and shrapnel strewn along the
railroad tracks.
In rapid succession there appeared fire trucks, ambulances,
helicopters, people from the FBI, TSB and TV news reporters, all
swarming about. Their flashing lights lit up the blustery night air.
There was also one tow truck, hoisting Danny's van out of the
ditch.

"Who was in the car, the one that got slammed?" a reporter asked
one of the firemen.
"Hard to tell." the fireman responded back. 'There ain't much left
out there."
Some reporters tried to crowd around Danny and Bill as they
made their way out of the surreal scene.
The young policeman led them out, running interference for the
beleaguered pair who were now wrapped in blankets to fend off
the falling temperatures.

Chapter 12

The forty ton crane lifted the large, packaged air conditioning
unit up over the edge of the roof.

Bill signaled the crane operator with his good hand while Danny
guided the unit into place.

He had some help from the other contractors he had subbed for
the job.

It was now over a week since the incident at the train tracks.

"So, no word on who was in the car yet?" Bill asked his boss.

"They think he was an antique dealer or something like that.
Probably a cover for something else. The contaminated devices
recovered from the malls, well, they are blaming them on
terrorism." Danny replied.

"Terrorism my ass," Bill shot back, "They blame everything on
terrorism anymore. That was some kind of conspiracy, you and I
both know it." Bill went on. "A conspiracy for drug companies to
make us sick so they can sell cold pills. An elaborate plan to keep
their stockholders fat and happy."

Danny smiled. "You sound like me now, ya know that?"

"That's starting to worry me too." Bill laughed.

"Anyway, all the leads went cold." Danny continued. "No paper trails, no hard evidence anywhere to be found, just some empty buildings and dead ends. I am not surprised in the least. It was set up that way from the beginning."
The crane gently set the unit down right in place.

That night, Danny and Liz went out to dinner to an Italian restaurant. They talked about normal things for a change, the kids, work, the weather, local news stories, sports. Danny still kept his eyes open for anything suspicious. But it was not to be. For him it was over.
As he lay in bed later that night he tossed and turned, thinking about a million things.
In the distance he heard his train approaching. The whistle got louder and then short bursts as it approached the crossing gates. He heard the rumble of the steel wheels as they rolled over the hardened track.
He wondered where it was going and who was on it. What kinds of lives did they lead working on a railroad, working in jobs that were very often passed down from father to son.
Then he saw his train hit the car that was chasing him.
 He wiped some sweat off his brow, closed his eyes and drifted off to sleep.

Somewhere in New Jersey a raspy voice made a late night phone call to a foreman who worked for the local water authority in Phoenix.
" I have another job for you" he said.

Bonus Story!

THE LAKEVIEW MANOR INCIDENT
By Ed Dice

Chapter 1

Dan Edwards had just stepped out of the shower. He was drying off and glanced at the full length mirror through the steam in the bathroom. "Not bad," he thought, "for an older guy anyway." As he made his way out of the temporary sauna he heard the phone ring, he yelled down, "don't answer that." Too late, his wife Liz had already picked it up. He heard some talking and when she came to the bottom of the stairs and yelled up, "Danny, it's for you," he cringed. They were suppose to go out to dinner with some friends in an hour. It was the first cold spell of the season and he had already put in a full day. The last thing he wanted to do was go out on another service call, not tonight. He stuck his head around the corner and said quietly, in case Liz hadn't muted the phone, "I'm not here."

Liz mouthed back to him, "it's Mrs. Horne, sorry." "Great, just fricking great," Dan mumbled under his breath. He grabbed the upstairs phone trying not to sound disgruntled. "Hey Mrs. Horne, what's going on." The older lady responded back, "it's not what going on Dan, it's what's not going on, as in my new furnace." she quipped back at him. "Its' going to get cold tonight," she went on, "I don't want my Smoochy to get sick."

She was an elderly widow, her husband now gone. She used a walker on occasion and really shouldn't be living alone but her independence was the only thing she had left in the world. She still drove her older white, Buick Riviera to the store and to church. Her kids had moved away and after her only sister had to be put in Sunnyside Village, a nice sounding name for a nursing home, she had little left save her tiny condo and her cat, Smoochy.

Smoochy was her companion. A long haired, white Persian cat that was obviously overfed and spoiled. The animal didn't care much for strangers as most Persians don't, but Smoochy liked Danny. When ever he was there the cat would brush against his legs or jump up and sit on his lap, he would return the affection and Mrs. Horne always noticed that and remarked about it. As frail as Mrs. Horne was physically, she still had her wits about her, as Danny knew full well. The Hornes had been his customer for many years when they still lived in the large, stone front home in an upscale part of town. Her kids urged her to sell the old house after dad died. Danny thinks they just wanted to get their hands on the profit from the sale of the eight bedroom colonial. Well she sold it alright, and for a tidy sum. The large home in the now trendy and highly desirable location sold for well into six figures. But much to her children's dismay, she put most of the money into investments and bought a small, seven room condo in a gated community. Lakeview Manor was a relatively newer development, and as the name says, near the lake. She didn't need 3 bedrooms but just in case her grandkids ever wanted to stay over, she would have room for them. They never did. Although her original furnace seemed fine, she had Dan over to look at it after she moved in. Being only 8 years old the thing already had a tiny crack in the heat exchanger, a serious and expensive flaw. Danny had seen it before, expensive new houses with builder grade equipment. Cheap stuff in the walls but attractive looking habitats to attract potential buyers, buyers who knew little about construction, nor cared about it. Danny would just shake his head but keep his comments to himself. It would only insult their intelligence if he told them how cheaply their new dream house was built. And what good would it do, it was too late anyway, they had already bought it. He had replaced the defective furnace with a much better unit, one with a higher efficiency and more reliable components.

"OK, Ms. Horne, I'll swing by and have a look see," Danny now realizing dinner would have to be postponed. The complex was not too far from where Danny lived and the furnace was only about a year old. Danny told his wife he had to go on this one and to call their friends and make the reservations for an hour later. He was sure it would be something simple and he would be home in no time. Liz frowned, but was used to it by now. After almost 30 years of this, she knew the deal.

Danny said jokingly , "Hey honey, I told you not to answer the phone didn't I?"

Of course he knew it was probably for the best. Had she not answered it, his cell phone would probably start ringing right in the middle of his first cold beer. Better to get it taken care of now. That, and he was already showered so all he had to do was change his clothes when he returned from the call. He could taste that first cold beer and nice steak meal as he got into his van. They hadn't been out with the O'Neals in quite some time and he looked forward to the fun night ahead. They were old friends going way back to the college years. After a few drinks they would end up laughing over the crazy times they had shared. There were only a few friends they had like that, ones you could really let down your hair with.

Yep, Danny would wrap up this call in 10 minutes, come hell or high water. If something was really amiss with that new unit, he had taken some portable electric heaters along for temporary heat until he could return the next day when he had more time. After all, he didn't want Smoochy to come down with an illness. He chuckled to himself thinking of the white Persian.

As fate would have it, Danny would not make that dinner, not tonight anyway. His furry friend, Smoochy, was getting colder. Danny's life was about to take an unexpected turn in the road. A turn he had little control over.

Mrs. Horne called the front gate, a voice answered, one unfamiliar to her. "Oh I was expecting Harv to pick up, this is Mrs. Horne up on 752 Sweet Gum." A caller ID setup at the gate assured the guard the call was indeed coming from a residence in the protected plan.

"Harv called in sick today ma'am. I'm filling in for him, can I help you?"

"Well yes" she reluctantly answered. Older people didn't like surprises, or any changes in the routine for that matter. "I am expecting a guy to arrive shortly and repair my furnace, his name is Dan Edwards, I assume he will be driving a work truck . OK?"

"Got it" the mystery voice replied, "will let him pass. Anything else?"

" Nope, that's all," and she hung up the receiver.

She then waited patiently by the large, bay window, sitting in her grandmother's Victorian style, chaise lounge, reading a large print, trashy novel by Danielle Steele.

Chapter 2

As Danny approached the gate to Lakeview Manor he put on his headlights. The days were slowly getting shorter now with the onset of winter. He saw something running near the entrance road. It was small and white, it darted behind a hedge. It looked like Smoochy. "Couldn't be" Danny remarked out loud, Smoochy was a house cat and he remembered Mrs. Horne saying how Smoochy wasn't fond of going outside. Besides it was getting colder and Mrs. Horne would never let the white Persian out with darkness approaching. Danny stopped at the gate and the guard asked, "Mr. Edwards, going to the Horne residence, right?" "That's me and I shouldn't be very long either. By the way, did you see a white cat running around here a minute ago? I think it was Mrs. Horne's cat, it's really strange it would be out now. " "Nope, didn't see a thing but if I do, I'll give a call" the young guard replied back, now sounding a little nervous for some reason.

Danny waved and headed up the street to 752 Sweet Gum. He pulled in the drive and down around the back of the two story condo. He lightly tapped the horn waiting for the garage door to open. He waited a minute and then tapped it again, a little longer this time. Usually she would open the garage door from a remote button upstairs. He knew she had to be home, maybe in the bathroom or something. At her age and with that walker, well, it could take some time. Then Danny noticed the back door to the condo a few feet away. Through the screen door, Danny could see that the main door was open. Now that was really odd, no way should that be opened. Like many old timers Mrs. Horne kept the place locked up tight, especially being allalone like that. Danny shut off the truck and went over to the door. He banged on it with his flashlight. He opened the screen door and yelled inside, "Ms Horne, I'm here.......for the furnace......hello....hello."

He went inside, it was dark and cold. He hit the switch by the back door but the lights didn't come on. He made his way past the game room and the bar, his flashlight flicked off and he smacked it. "Stupid thing" he said out loud, "hello, Ms Horne, anyone here?" Smacking the flashlight again, he suddenly tripped over a small end table and went head over heels. He hit the ground hard and the flashlight went flying. It landed on the tile floor and came back to life, rolling gently to a stop. From the beam of the light Danny could now make out something that sent chills through every nerve in his body. Mrs. Horne, sprawled out at the bottom of the stairs. Her walker, a twisted piece of chrome and plastic lay beneath her. Blood was pooled under her bluish gray hair on the hard tile floor.

"Oh my God" Danny repeated over and over as he made for the flashlight and then on to Mrs. Horne. He bent down to see if she was still breathing, she wasn't. Her eyes were rolled back in her head, her eyelids open. Danny fumbled for his cell phone from his jacket pocket. He was in a panic, he grabbed the phone and immediately dropped it, he was a wreck. As he picked up the phone he heard a noise in the back room, near the furnace. His heart raced, a beam from the flashlight swinging over that way revealed a quickly moving shadow. Or so it seemed. He yelled out, "Help…….anyone there……"He moved slowly towards it, the heavy, black steel flashlight gripped tightly in his hand, now also a weapon. He relaxed as Smoochy came running out of the back hallway.

"C'mere little buddy" Danny cooed, "Come on, over here." Danny picked up the white Persian and sat down on the steps above the deceased Mrs. Horne, finally calming down a bit. He dialed 911. Danny jumped as he heard the back screen door close. He took a few steps and shone the light that way, nothing. "Perhaps the wind," he thought, "maybe the self closing mechanism was jammed and it was just now shutting." His mind raced, the operator answered, "911 emergency operator, how may we help you?"

As Danny waited for the EMT's and police he wondered how long Mrs. Horne had been dead, should he have tried CPR? It was obvious that it would have been no use, she was clearly dead with a traumatic head injury and who knows what else, no movement, no breathing, no sign of life. At her age, a fall like that was easily fatal, and probably better than had she survived it. Danny had watched his dad wither away and die and wouldn't wish that same fate on anyone.

Danny then decided to get the basement lights on. He saw it was track lighting over the bar and some recessed ceiling lights throughout the rest of the room. Surely all the bulbs weren't bad. Neither switch worked down there. He made his way back to the breaker panel in the mechanical area, near the furnace. He shone his light and saw the bottom left breaker was off, not tripped, but switched off. He pushed it back to the on position and the lights were back. "OK, that's good" he said aloud. Then he heard the furnace come to life also. "So that is why the house was cold," he wondered, now talking to Smoochy as well as himself. "Why would this breaker be off?" Smoochy paid him no mind and was now examining his late owner.

Was it overloaded somehow? He wondered why, if it was overloaded it would have been in the tripped position, but it was off. Smoochy was now licking Mrs. Horne's face in an effort to get her to respond. Danny picked up the feline and walked over by the bar and sat down. "I'm afraid she is gone now Smoochy, off to a better place." Then he noticed some dirt and tiny green leaves in the cat's fur on his underbelly. Smoochy had been outside after all, it was indeed Smoochy Danny had seen on his way in. So how did he get out and more importantly, how did he get back in? Danny pondered all these questions as he heard the ambulance approach. He walked over by the back door, went out still holding the cat and walked up around to the front of the condo.

As he waited, he called his wife and briefly told her what took place. Liz would have to reschedule dinner with their old friends.

That was the last thing on Danny's mind right now though, he had other things to worry about.

The coroner's wagon pulled in the drive. The EMT's were packing up, nothing more to do here, Mrs. Horne was long gone. A small crowd of onlookers had gathered, neighbors who saw the commotion. The police had called in a detective, just to be sure. Jim Wadell had been on the force for some 25 years, working his way up from traffic to beat cop finally to detective. He was a no nonsense guy, not easily fooled. He asked Danny, "OK one more time. She called you to come and repair the furnace around 6 PM, Is that right?"

"Yes, around that time, I was getting ready to go out to dinner with some friends, just got out of the shower. My wife answered and I really didn't want to be home, if you know what I mean. But she was a long time customer and I knew she would ...."Danny was cut off by the detective in mid sentence, "OK then, so what time did you get here, I can check the gate log later but around what time was it?"

"I would say around 7 or so, it was getting dark and........"The Detective pressed on, "Did you see anyone or anything suspicious when you arrived?"

"Well now that you mention it, I swear I saw Mrs Horne's cat running around down by the front gate when I pulled up, and that cat almost never goes out. She would never let Smoochy out with darkness approaching and getting colder like it is now. Plus the cat hated to be outside"

"Smoochy?' The detective asked rolling his eyes. "Smoochy is her cat's name?

"Yeah, why?" Danny asked.

"Oh nothing, I guess, Smoochy..... OK, so Smoochy was outside and you saw him and then?" the detective not too concerned about her cat slipping outside, after all it was just a cat.

"Well," Danny went on, "Funny thing is, when I got here, and after I found Mrs. Horne.... like that, I heard some noise in the back room. It kind of freaked me out, I was afraid someone else was in here. Then Smoochy came running out. And later I noticed some dirt and tiny leaves on his underbelly. So if the cat was outside, then how did it get back in, and why?"

"I don't know about that" the grim detective responded, "Not sure it really matters, perhaps a window or the old lady opened the door a crack. Maybe someone came to the door and the cat ran out, who knows?

At this point, it looks like a fall. An accident, plain and simple. Happens all the time, these old folks living all alone. Sometimes no one notices they were missing for days. We get a call from a paperboy or mailman. We get permission to enter and find them, hard as a rock. And the smell, wow. If she hadn't called you for the furnace she may have laid here for quite some time. I checked upstairs, no sign of a struggle, no forced entry, her jewelry seems to be intact in the box on her dresser. There is even a large jar of coins in her cupboard, old ones too. And a couple $20's practically sticking out of her purse, in plain view. If someone was in here and did this, what would the motive be? Nope, can't see it. I am writing this up as I see it, an accident, a tragic accident. Do you know if she has any kin?" the Detective asked Danny who was now in a daze staring at the corpse as the coroner covered it. "Um, yeah, she has a couple kids, they live out of state, one is in New York I think, not sure about the other one."

"OK, we'll track them down and let them know." the detective now putting his note pad away.

"We have your number if we need you for anything else. So, that cat seems to like you. You want to take it home for now, if not, I'll call animal control and they will stick the critter in a cage somewhere, until the kids get here. It's up to you, either way."

Danny was still in a trance, the words seemed to be coming out of the detective's mouth and going right by him.

"Hey, ya want the cat or not?" the detective now getting a little antsy.

"Oh…..yeah, sure. I'll take him for now, no problem. Am I done here officer?"

"Here is my card," detective Wadell said, handing it to Danny, "call me if you think of anything else, anything important I mean." Danny was about to tell him about the breaker being off but thought better of it. At this point he was ready to get out of there and go home. He found Smoochy's litter box and grabbed the large bag of litter nearby and headed out to his truck. He would swing by a 7-11 on the way home and get a few cans of cat food. He put Smoochy on a drop cloth he had on the truck, sitting on the floor of the passenger's side. As he started to pull out an old couple came up to his truck. "Oh poor Mrs. Horne" they said, "what happened." Danny quickly filled them in, he was in no mood to elaborate." The older gentleman looked down and saw the cat. "Oh there is Smoochy, she never let him out of her sight you know. Funny thing though. About an hour ago I saw the cat running through our yard. Then awhile later I noticed the new gate guard bringing him back up, along the trail way down there. He seemed to be hurrying and he had a hooded sweatshirt on covering his head. It seemed odd. I knew it was him because as he turned up towards the condo, he got out his cell phone. He pulled down the hood for a minute, seemed to be talking to someone, then he pulled his hood back up and continued on. I lost him when he got up there near those trees. The guards are not suppose to leave the gate between 7 AM and 11 PM, unless they have a replacement, but once in a great while they do, but not for long. For overnight access and short time periods to go the john and such, the residents use a special code to open the gate, on that keypad by the guard shack. And there are security cameras that monitor every vehicle that enters and leaves." The old man going into more detail than Danny wanted to know.

"Oh well, I guess he decided to do a good deed and return the cat, not sure why he brought it back that way, down near the lake. It is a roundabout way."

Danny looked at the old couple in amazement. "The guard, who is new here you say, brought the cat back up tonight? How did he know whose cat it was, I mean if he was new to the job?"

The old man looked puzzled, "I don't know, maybe Mrs. Horne called the gate after the cat got out, that's all I can figure out."

Danny's head was spinning now, he didn't want to think about it any more.

He had just been through quite an ordeal but what was to come was even more bizarre.

As he pulled out of the plan, he stopped at the gate. The young guard said, "Wow, big goings on up there, I heard the old lady died, too bad."

"Yes it is, and I am the one that found her. Pretty sad, and now I get to take the cat home. My wife is allergic to cats too, so I don't know," Danny replied, and then continued. "So the cat got out and you brought it back up to her huh?" The guard got a look in his eyes and tensed up. "No sir, not me, we are not allowed to leave the gate, except for a couple very short breaks, company policy. Whoever told you that, they must be mistaken."

Danny was not about to argue, at this point he didn't care. The old couple may have been wrong, it was getting dark. The guard may be lying to cover up the fact that he left the gate, against company policy. All he knew was he wanted to get home now and forget it. He called Liz and said, "I'll be home in about 20 minutes, I have to swing by the store and pick up some cat food. It's been a long night, I'm exhausted, and starving."

Liz said, "So you are going to eat cat food?"

Now Danny started laughing, the tension gave way to hysteria. He was laughing so hard tears started to form. "What are you talking about Dan?" Liz now also starting to chuckle, "are you alright?"

"Yeah, I'm fine" the laughter now subsiding some, "I am bringing you home a present though, you won't believe it."

"What" Liz wanted to know, her curiosity piquing, "what kind of present, what are you talking about, you sure you're OK?"

"I'm fine, see you in a few," Danny now making a turn into the convenience store.

"Call Papa Johns pizza. Order a large cheese or something." Danny went on, "I'll stop by on the way home and pick it up."

"OK , sounds better than cat food," Liz said, "I'll call right now so it will be ready, bye."

The young security guard took out his cell phone and made a call.
"We may have a little problem here."
"What kind of problem?" came the reply.
"Probably nothing, nothing at all. That stupid cat, it's all his fault,
and that repairman. Like I said, it's most likely nothing," the
young guard now showing a darker side of his personality.
"It better be nothing." the voice on the other end came back, "it
damn well better be nothing."

120

Chapter 3

Danny burst through the door and yelled up the stairs, "Hey pizza man is here, come get it."

He secretly put Smoochy in the basement. He would break it to her later, first he wanted to tell his story, and what a wild story it was. They had the Pizza, Danny downed a few cold beers to go with it. He went over the series of events, leaving out nothing except for the part about bringing home the cat. He told Liz he was suspicious at first, of the guard and the conflicting stories, but let it go.

He often read into things too much for his own good. All the conspiracy theories and urban legends out there. Most of them bunk, people looking for excitement is all.

Liz shook her head, "Wow, that is really sad, poor thing dying all alone like that. Maybe if you had arrived there sooner, who knows?"

"Yeah," Danny agreed, "Life is funny like that, is it fate or do little things mean the difference between life and death? Like when you wrecked the car last month. If you left the house even 30 seconds later, you wouldn't have run into that UPS truck. Who knows how many times you avoided accidents though, by leaving when you did. Or going the certain route that you took."

Liz looked at him funny. "Not just you hon, I mean everyone. If this stuff is fate then no matter when or what, things are destined to occur. I guess we will never know, not sure I want to either."

The beer was kicking in some now. "She had a good, long life, that's all anyone can really ask for. We all take our turn at tragedy, it is the nature of our existence. And we all end up in the same place. I suppose the journey is just as important as the destination." Danny cracked open another beer. "Yep, all things considered, it could have been worse. Look at the young kids dying, or people suffering in third world countries, many of them never have much of a life. Mrs. Horne had what many people only dream of. Oh well, that reminds me dear, speaking of things she had." Danny preparing Liz for the white ball of fur whom he spotted sticking his paw under the door from the basement stairs." One thing she had was a cat. A beautiful white Persian. She loved that thing, spoiled it rotten, hardly ever went outside."

"So?" Liz replied.

"Well, you see, in the mayhem that followed, I somehow, um. Well this cop asked me if I would, just till her kids get there........"

"What Dan, spit it out." At that moment Liz glanced and saw the tiny paw reaching out below the door into the kitchen.

"AEEEEEEE," she yelled and jumped up on the table. "A MOUSE," she screamed." GET IT, HIT IT WITH YOUR SHOE!!"

"Relax," Danny now laughing, "It's not a mouse," and he opened the door. Smoochy was perched on the top step, he looked up at both of them and tilted his head ever so slightly.

Liz climbed down off the table, calming down now she said, "Aww, how cute." She paused, thinking for just a second.

"So you got her precious cat did you? What's his name or is it a her?"

"It's a he, and his name is, ready for this?" At this point she was ready for just about anything.

"His name is Smoochy. That's why I said I had to stop for cat food. Not because I was delirious."

Danny opened yet one more beer. Liz said, "Make me a drink will you, I think I need one too. You know I have allergies to cats, well I did many years ago anyway. I would imagine I still do unless I was somehow miraculously cured and didn't know it. Which I seriously doubt."

Danny responded, "It's just until her kids arrive, didn't want to see the poor thing in a shelter. Mrs. Horne would hate that, I'm sure. We can keep it in the basement for now, shouldn't be much of a problem, do you think?"

Liz, taking a sip of her cherry flavored vodka, "It should be OK I guess. I hope I don't start sneezing or scratching. He is really precious though. I don't have much choice anyway, at this point, do I now?" They finished their drinks and had a few more laughs over the day's events. Liz headed upstairs.

Danny took the cat down to the basement, he got the littler box ready and opened up some cat food.

It was a nicer, finished basement. He left on a light for Smoochy and went up to bed himself. It had been a long day, he was drained, both mentally and physically.

On Sunday, Danny checked the obits and the funeral was on Wednesday.

He decided to pass on that but would stop by the funeral home one night and pay his respects. He would also tell Mrs. Horne's kids about her cat and figure out what to do with him.

The parking lot at Myers Funeral Home was not very crowded. Danny pulled in the lot and made his way to the viewing area. He hated funeral homes, he kept thinking about his parents and how tough that was.

Seeing them die was bad enough but then to end up lying in a coffin in some stranger's house with a bunch of people making small talk and saying how good they looked. He wondered how we ever came up with this bizarre custom anyway.

As he entered he tried to pick out the surviving children. He had seen them occasionally, years ago when they lived in the big house. From what he could remember they were spoiled brats. Perhaps time had changed them. He went up to Julie first, she was the oldest. He guessed she was now probably in her early 30's. A few kids were running around at her feet, the grandkids he decided. He introduced himself and gave his condolences.

"Sorry about your Mom," he said. "She was a fine lady. It was really tragic. I guess the police told you I was the one that found her. Really sad."

"Yes it is," she retorted. "We told her to get a companion, she could have, you know. She was so stubborn. Well, it's too late now. Thanks for all you did Mr. Edwards."

Then she turned to chase after her youngest daughter who by now was literally bored to tears. Not only was she tired of having to stand around in a pink dress and try to behave, her older brother was poking her on the back.

"Quit it," she said to her kids. "Can't you be good for 5 minutes." Then she delivered her troublemaker son to his father and took her daughter into the bathroom.

Danny approached the son now, he would tell him about the cat.

"Remember me," he said reaching out his hand.

"Yeah, Edwards, the furnace guy. I understand you are the one that found mom?" Mrs. Horne's only other child, Robert, was a businessman of some sort. Danny didn't know exactly what he did, nor did he care.

"My condolences to you and your family," Danny pronounced.

"Thanks, but it is probably for the best," Robert replied, matter of factly.

That sort of took Danny by surprise, the way he said it.

"I suppose so," Danny agreeing thinking about how his own dad had suffered for several years before passing on.

"Not sure if anyone told you," Danny now seizing the moment to bring up Smoochy.

"But I have her cat. There was no one else around that night, the policeman asked me if I wanted to hold on to it until........."

Robert cut him off, "That stupid cat, so that's where it went? I never liked that damn thing," he went on.

"As far as I am concerned, you can have it. Do whatever, if you don't want it, take it to the pound, or toss it off a bridge. My sister won't want it either, her kids are allergic to everything under the sun." Robert's older boy was now getting involved with Julie's son, who was bored that his sister was out of reach.

"Knock it off," Robert yelled, rather loud for such an environment.

"Who are you yelling at?" came the reply from Julie as she emerged from the bathroom, practically dragging her daughter along by the arm.

"Can't you raise your kids?" Robert miffed at Julie.

"It ain't my kid, it's yours, just like his old man." She replied in a nasty tone.

As they quieted down but continued with their discussion of child rearing, Danny moved away and eased up to the coffin. Under his breath he said, "Take care ma'am. I'll make sure your Smoochy is provided for."

He blessed himself and disappeared from the well lit room that smelled like flowers.

"What a bunch of idiots," Danny said to Liz when he returned home. "They haven't changed at all. Now they are spoiled adults with little brats of their own to boot. I know our kids weren't always perfect but trust me, they were nothing like that bunch."

"And the cat?" Liz asked, "what about the cat?"

"That might be a bit of a problem," Danny mused.

"Seems neither of the kids want it, matter of fact, they apparently hated it. Her son told me to toss it off a bridge. The daughters kids have more allergies than you do."

"Danny," Liz said in a special tone she saved for just such occasions.

"Listen," he came back. "I will find someone, give me a few days. One of my customers has some cats, she will take in another one, considering the circumstances. I'm sure. And, well, I kind of promised Mrs. Horne I would make sure Smoochy is provided for."

Liz looked at him and paused.

"Great, well in that case you better go down and feed him and clean out the litter box too. I'm going to get some Benadryl, just in case."

The day after the funeral Danny's phone rang.

"Edwards mechanical" he answered as usual.

"I'm looking for a Daniel Edwards," came the reply.

Great Danny thought, and he almost hung up on him, another salesman. They always call around 9 AM and they ask for you by name.

"Who is this?" Danny shot back, ready to slam down the phone.

"This is Greg Halmon, I'm the attorney handling the estate of the late Mrs. Horne. Are you Mr. Edwards?"

Danny now perked up not knowing what to think.

"Yes, that's me."

"As executor of Mrs. Horne's estate I am having a reading of the will this afternoon. Can you attend? I know it's short notice but she stipulated it to take place immediately after her funeral. I'm thinking around 3 PM? Would that be good for you Mr. Edwards?"

"Why do you want me to be there? Because I am the one who discovered her or something?"

All sorts of things were going through his head.

"Mr. Edwards, you are listed a beneficiary, can you make it at 3?"

"Yes, I suppose I can," came his reply.

"And you do have possession of Mrs. Horne's cat, Smoochy? The police said you took it home temporarily."

The lawyer went on, "Can you bring the cat along? I know it's an unusual request."

"Well, OK, I can bring the cat, but why?" Danny guessing that someone at the reading will would take Smoochy off his hands as per Mrs. Horne's request.

"Mr. Edwards, at this point all I can tell you is it's in your best interest to attend, and to bring the cat."

"Very well, what is the address?" More crazy thoughts raced through Danny's mind as he jotted it down.

"See you at 3 PM" and he hung up the phone.

As Danny entered the lawyer's office he felt out of place. The two offspring of Mrs. Horne sat at opposite sides of the conference table. They both had a look of shock on their faces as Danny walked in, holding the cat no less.

"What the heck is he doing here?" asked Robert.

Julie just stared in disbelief.

"Please take a seat and lets get this done," said the attorney.

The cat was a little fidgety, Danny held him tight as he could without hurting him.

Julie and Robert started bickering over some antique furniture left in the condo.

The lawyer called them to attention once again.

"OK, lets see here."

And he began. First he asked names and addresses of those in attendance. He verified some personal information about them and some other legalese.

"To each of her grandchildren, Roberta Horne has left the amount of $250,000 each. To be put in a trust fund for them until they reach legal age, at which time it is to be turned over solely to them."

Robert and Julie smiled, anxious to hear what they would get considering the large amount each of their children got.

"To each of her two children, the sum of $5000 each and all my other worldly possessions which I am sure they are already fighting over."

Their smiles turned to bewilderment.

The attorney went on.

"And to my cat, Smoochy, the only true friend I have left in the world, I leave the bulk of my investments, savings and cash on hand, minus funeral expenses and attorney fees.

And in so doing I leave my cat Smoochy to the only person I ever met who treated him nicely and in turn the only person Smoochy ever cared for, Mr. Daniel Edwards. I also leave Mr. Edwards in sole charge of that inheritance to do with as he pleases as long as he keeps Smoochy safe and sound and treats him as I have in the past."

Robert and Julie went ballistic, "WHAT, that is insane" Robert yelled. "For once in his life Bob is right," replied Julie. "We will fight this in probate court 'til hell freezes over," Robert screamed, "Mom was obviously nuts, anyone can see that. How do we know this furnace guy didn't brainwash or threaten her?" Robert was losing control now. "No way, this is insanity, a cat? A cat gets mom's estate??"
"Calm down" said the attorney, until I finish.
"Your mom knew exactly what she was doing, trust me. Mr. Edwards had no idea about any of this, it was totally up to Mrs. Horne."
"NO WAY" Julie now yelling.
As they continued on with their threats the lawyer read more.
"I am to monitor the possession and treatment of Smoochy. Should Smoochy pass on before Mr. Edwards, which is of course very likely, the inheritance is Mr. Edwards to do with as he pleases."
The late Mrs. Horne's kids were now even fighting with themselves, asking how could they let this happen. As they drowned each other out with accusations and threats, Danny holding his new, furry friend up on his shoulder asked, "Just how much money did she leave us, I mean me and Smoochy?"
Attorney Halmon replied, "Well the final figure isn't in and won't be for some time. As of right now, I would guess in the neighborhood of two and a half million dollars, give or take a hundred thousand or so."
Danny had to sit down. He was immune to the yelling and screaming going on behind him. His heart rate increased, he began to feel light headed. The cat purred and licked his face. The attorney asked him, "Can I get you a drink? You look pale. I have some soda or water here."
"Anything stronger?" Danny asked back, in a state of shock.

The lawyer pulled a bottle out of his desk drawer and poured Danny a double over some ice cubes from his small office sized fridge.

As he downed the whiskey he heard Robert bellowing, "I loved that cat, everyone knows that. I am contacting my lawyer immediately. That cat is mine, we were tricked."

Danny finished off the drink. The attorney grinned at him, shaking his head as if justice had been served.

Danny decided it was time to get out of there, as he left the lawyers office, someone was sitting on a bench out in the hallway. It was detective Wadell. He said, "Mr. Edwards, so I see you still have the cat. Can I talk to you for a minute?"

Chapter 4

Danny cautiously made his way over and sat down by the
detective.
"Yes, what is it?"
The detective began.
"Seems you made out pretty good in that deal huh? That's a lot of
money to suddenly come into, isn't it?
I want to go over the events again with you. I'm not so sure it
was indeed an accident. Now what time did you arrive at Mrs.
Hornes?

"Am I a suspect in something now?" Danny asked in bewilderment.

"I had no idea she was going to leave me the cat or any money or anything, ask the lawyer, he will tell you. I tried to explain from the start that I thought I saw the cat running loose as I pulled into the condo complex. And there was an older couple who swore they saw the young guard carrying Smoochy up towards Mrs. Hornes. And he was taking a round about way, down by the lake. And the kids, what about them, they thought they were going to inherit the dough, not me. Go question them. It ain't right to be........." Danny's voice getting louder and more confused. The detective cut him off.' Now calm down Mr. Edwards. I didn't accuse you, or anyone for that matter, of any crime. Lets just say for right now you are a person of interest. And its' probably best to take a formal statement from you, perhaps down at the station, say tomorrow morning?"

"A STATEMENT, down at the STATION? That sure sounds like someone is in big trouble." Danny getting excited, went on. "This is ridiculous, I didn't ask for the cat or the money, hell you were the one who suggested I take him home to begin with, remember?"

"Yes, I know," Detective Wadell agreed. "Like I said, all we want to do is fill in the blanks here. There was quite a bit of money left in her estate. We have to make absolutely sure that no crime was committed, that's all. Come in around 9 AM, it won't take longer than an hour, promise. OK? You still have my card, the address in on it."

"Whatever, I have nothing to hide," Danny relenting. "I'll be there."

As the detective left, Danny stuck his head back inside the lawyer's office and asked, "Excuse me, Mr. Halmon, do you do criminal law too?"

"No, but I know quite a few who do," the Lawyer replied. "Let me get you a number. The detective was here earlier, snooping around. I had to tell him about the inheritance, but I assured him you had no prior knowledge. Don't worry, you have nothing to worry about. Do you Mr. Edwards?"

Danny looked him right in the eye. "Nothing, nothing at all."

"Good, I didn't think so, you ain't the type. Anyway, here is a card, this guy is very good, give him a call, mention my name. He will tell you whether you need his services or not. Now I have to go back over there and try to explain to the kids why their mom left her estate largely to her cat and her furnace man. Should be fun."

The counselor turned and walked back over to the feuding Horne children, he was trying to clarify the situation as Danny turned and left his office.

Danny stormed into his house and found his wife up in the bedroom getting changed.

"You just ain't going to believe this."

"Danny" she said, "please, the cat, can you put him in the basement dear?"

"Yeah, this cat, Smoochy. One minute he is worth a zillion dollars and the next he is causing me to spend the rest of my life in jail." Danny babbled.

"Whatever are you talking about hon?" Liz asked.

"You just ain't going to believe it, nope. I can't believe it, how can anyone else?"

Danny took Smoochy down to the basement, gave him some food and put on the TV for him to watch.

He grabbed a beer on his way back upstairs. Liz was getting dressed. He said, "Sit down, and get ready for the story of all stories." He drank the beer in 2 gulps and told Liz how:

1. They are suddenly millionaire's, and.

2. Her loving husband of 30 years was now a prime suspect in a murder case.

Liz was at a loss for words. Her mouth dropped open in disbelief. Danny went into the details and said he was going to call the lawyer and see what he thought.

Liz grabbed Danny tight, and said, "Don't worry Dan, this will all get straightened out in the morning. You have nothing to worry about. I'm sure it is just a formality. After they get done talking to you they will see you couldn't hurt a fly. As far as the money, who cares. We have a wonderful life together. Money isn't going to change that. There is no reason for them to think you would ever do such a thing. Now relax and call the lawyer, he will put your mind at ease."

" I suppose you're right," Danny confessed. "I just have these images of them sitting me under a hot light bulb and cross examining me until I pass out. Maybe I watch too many police shows or something. Of course on the bright side, that cat did just change our whole life, in an instant. We can move to a big house, with a pool and a hot tub. You can get that large, walk in closet you always wanted. I can get a Porsche.

Our kids will be taken care of for the rest of their lives as well."

"Danny," Liz interrupted him, "Like I said, we are good the way we are. We have great kids who love us. Money is only a means to an end. As long as we have our health, we are the richest people on earth."

"Yeah, I know," Danny agreed, "I guess sometimes it's so easy to forget what you do have. I'm going to call the lawyer now."

Danny called the attorney and explained the situation. The lawyer advised him to have counsel, just in case. He instructed Danny to let him handle it. He would call the detective and set up a time for them to take their statement. And it wouldn't be tomorrow at 9 AM either. First Danny and his lawyer would meet and go over the events. He had seen police take advantage of innocent people before, confusing them and offering deals. Nope, that wasn't going to happen this time.

Danny felt much better after his phone call. He thought how everyone makes fun of lawyers and puts them down, until they need one that is. Then they are the greatest people you ever want to meet.

Danny and Liz had dinner. He wanted to forget about his day, it was too exhausting to go over it anymore. They discussed her job, as a high school teacher she always had plenty of good stories. Things that distracted them both from the Hornes, and Smoochy and the money were a welcome change.

After dinner, Danny attended to the white Persian downstairs. He cleaned out the litter box, freshened up the water and then sat down on the couch nearby. Smoochy jumped up on his lap. The TV was on and some mindless show about Hollywood celebrities filled the screen. Danny clicked the remote. "Bad boys, bad boys , whatcha gonna do, whatcha gonna do when they come for you" came over the speakers.

Danny was certainly not in the mood to watch Cops right now. He quickly changed it and found a program examining how UFO's have been visiting mankind since the stone age. He left it on and sat back on the comfy sofa. Smoochy was purring in his lap.

Some time passed and Danny finally muttered,

"What am I going to do about all this Smooch, huh? What the hell am I going to do?"

"Well for one thing, have the flatfoot check the gate log at the condo and the time of the 911 call. Even that idiot can figure out it didn't give you much time to kill someone, now did it?"

Danny shrieked out loud, "Who said that?"

He jumped up holding the cat and looked around. No one was there.

"And find out about that punk of a guard and what was he doing carrying me home right about then"

Danny looked down at Smoochy. In amazement, he listened as Smoochy went on.

"No, it wasn't any accident, that's for sure. Tell Dick Tracy to check and see about the new safe Ms. Horne just had installed in her basement. The one hidden down under the floor. The one that she kept for special occasions, hiding almost $250,000 dollars in it. Old people didn't completely trust banks, everyone knows that."

Danny sat back down and put Smoochy on one side of the couch. "Continue if you will Mr. Smoochy" he replied in disbelief. "Personally, it ain't all that hard to figure out. It was an inside job. The safe company was in cahoots with the guys at the guard company. They waited till she loaded the safe, then sneaked in and did the dirty deed. My poor Bobby, she didn't have a chance. They turned off the breaker, when she finally came to investigate down there, they tripped her down the dark stairs. That's why they left the coins, jewelry and cash in place. So it would look like an accident. What they didn't count on was her furnace going off when they killed the breaker for the downstairs lights causing you to show up unexpectedly. And they didn't expect me to escape. Bobby talked too much, to perfect strangers sometimes, she had no one else. She told the guys installing her new safe all about it. Why she wanted it hidden under the floor because of how much money she planned on keeping in it. So sad." Smoochy was now getting teary eyed.

"Danny, you coming up soon?" Danny waking from his cat nap, flew off the couch on hearing Liz.
"What the hell?" he said aloud. He shook his head and pushed his hair back. He looked at the cat, sitting there watching aliens invade Mexico. "Smoochy," he said, "Did you just…….I mean…..can you…..is it possible that………?? No, can't be, can it?"
It was a dream, a weird dream but still just a dream. The cat ignored him intent on the small beings with large eyes who moved on from Mexico to Texas.
Danny made his way up to bed and considered what Smoochy told him in his sleep. And you know what, it all made sense, as much sense as anything else that happened all week, that's for sure.
But was it merely a bizarre dream? How could the crazy safe story be proved, and how could he tell his lawyer or the police detective about it without sounding completely insane? At this point he considered that perhaps he was indeed going insane.

Chapter 5

Danny considered his options. Is it possible the story Smoochy told him was real? How could it be? Some kind of outer body experience maybe. Stranger things have happened he told himself. If he tells the police about it somehow, they could check cell phone records, receipts from the contractors who installed the safe, bank records and etc. They could also verify the guards story and the security tapes from the gate shack that day as well. But how could he tell them he found out from a talking cat, one who only talks to you in your sleep? They would most likely think he was nuts, maybe crazy enough to kill someone even. No, if he tells them things like that they will start to believe he knew about the safe and the money and that would actually make him more suspicious. The police would assume Danny knocked off Mrs. Horne to get the money from the safe. Money that no one else knew about.

Danny also considered just saying nothing. They have no case on me he figured. He showed up to fix the furnace, found her dead, immediately called 911, end of story. The fact he inherited over two million dollars was unknown to him, the lawyer for the estate was the only one who knew. He could testify to that. But what if the detective surmised that Mrs. Horne actually did tell Danny beforehand? How could he prove his story?

His head was spinning as he finally fell asleep. He dreamt he was in prison, working in the kitchen cafeteria, serving piles of slop food to dangerous looking inmates. One of the nastiest looking prisoners, a large bald headed, tattooed individual, who accused him of serving dead cats for dinner. He chased Danny through the dining area and cornered him in the recreation area where Danny had to fight for his life. He saw the inmate pull out a prison shiv and slowly come toward him. Danny awoke in a cold sweat and couldn't go back to sleep for nearly 2 hours. Even then he tossed and turned worrying about his predicament.

The phone rang at 9 a.m. the next morning causing Danny to jump out of bed.

"Hello, err I mean Edwards Mechanical."

"Is this Mr. Edwards?" a voice came over the receiver.

"Yes who is this" replied Danny wiping his eyes.

"This is Jim Barnes from Premiere Investing, we do financial planning, mutual funds, retirements, things of that nature. I understand you came into quite a large amount of capital recently."

"How did you know that?" Danny asked back. "Come to think of it, never mind, I can guess. Bye."

And Danny hung up. His phone rang the rest of the morning with all types of salesmen eager to get their share of Danny's new nest egg. As if he didn't have enough trouble, now he would be pestered by every kind of snake oil salesman on the planet. He made some coffee and settled down a bit and then called his new friend, his lawyer. They set up a meeting later that morning. After that they would go to the police and make a formal statement. The lawyer wanted Danny to get all his ducks in a row before he talked to the detective.

Danny decided to go check out the new Porsches before the meeting with the lawyer, just to take his mind off things. He would pass on his service calls to his only full time employee, Bill Strathmore.

Bill was ex Army. He was into computer programming at the Pentagon before the "incident" caused him to be honorably discharged. Danny never knew exactly what happened but he got the impression it was not made public, for many reasons. Bill liked to joke about it from time to time but never fully explained the situation at the Pentagon. All Danny knew was Bill could do practically anything with a computer and his background was very useful in troubleshooting newer control systems. After his stint in the service, Bill went to HVAC school and worked for his uncle doing refrigeration before he hooked up with Edwards

Mechanical. Danny was glad to have him too, he was a hard working, honest, clean cut young man. Bill Strathmore was also extremely reliable. He had a longtime, live in girlfriend and a daughter with her. She was 5 years old. Bill was planning on marrying her mother the following summer and finally giving his beautiful baby girl his name. She was the love of his life. They both were.

Danny met Bill for breakfast. He had already told him the story about Mrs. Horne's death and how he had found her on the emergency service call. Now he added the part about being a millionaire as well as a murder suspect. He asked Bill, "Can you use those high tech computer skills you have to find out some things for me? Like, could you somehow determine if someone recently had a secret safe installed in their basement and then took a large amount of money out of the bank and put it there?"

"Umm, well I suppose, if I had enough information, why?" Bill asked.

Danny told him about the dream and the talking cat.

Bill burst into laughter, "You're kidding me, right? Smoochy the cat told you that in a dream, while he was watching a show on UFO's? You got your Freon caps screwed down tight old man?" Danny shot back.

"Look, I know it's hard to imagine, but the whole thing is ridiculous if you think about it. So here is her name, address, the name of her bank and the amount of money supposedly in it. Oh yeah, and here is the name of the security company who guards Lakeviw Manor. Let me know if you find anything out."

"Why don't you just go take another nap with the cat, and ask him?' Bill joked in return.

"Very funny Mr. Strathmore," Danny said, "actually that isn't a bad idea, I just may do that."

He gave Bill the work orders for the next couple days and asked him to handle them,

"Call me if you get stuck Bill, OK? And one more thing I want you to think about William" And Danny never called him William. "When this whole inheritance thing gets done and if I do end up with a large wad of dough out of it, well, I've been thinking.

I may just pass this entire business on to someone else. Someone younger and energetic with new ideas to give it a fresh start. I have about had enough of it anyway, besides I won't really need to go bust my ass anymore. Are you interested? My kids have their own careers, they want no part of this little gig. It would be a shame to just let it die."

Bill was speechless for the first time in his life. "Thanks Danny, you know I am. It would be perfect for me and my family. How could I ever thank you, I mean........."

Danny cut him off, "Hey, you got some work orders there, better get going." With that, Danny grabbed the check, paid for breakfast, turned and walked out of the small diner.

****

Dan clicked save and closed out the MS Word document. He pushed himself away from the computer. He was tired of writing and it was too nice out to be sitting in his office. He was getting second thoughts about writing a book, a stupid mystery novel at that. What did he know about writing books anyway? How many millions of people had written books, taking up room in the back of bookstores? Silly books no one ever reads ending up in the Dollar stores and flea markets. And that's if they were lucky, most writers were never even published. Why bother he thought, why bother at all. But ever since his visit to the doctor last month his life had changed. A small dark spot on the MRI showed what was most likely a tumor, and with that tumor came the distinct threat of cancer. Since that day he had decided to finally commit to his dream of writing a book, while he still had the chance. He would write something using his career and life experiences as a backdrop. He certainly had enough material. But it was harder than he had imagined and took up way more time. And time was now his enemy, once an unlimited resource, it was suddenly a valuable commodity.

He went outside on his deck and sat in the sun under a beautiful blue sky.

Dan closed his eyes and thought back to the day he first painted his name and phone number on the side of a truck and drove around like a wayfaring vagabond trying to eek out a living for him and his family. What was he thinking? But in the end he had managed to pull it off, he was not sure how though.

Now all those years seemed like a whirlwind to him. Where had they gone? It seemed he had suddenly turned around one day and his kids were grown up with lives of their own, his hair was graying, his muscles sagged and he moved a little bit slower every single day. But he knew this was how it always happened, it was just harder when it was his turn. The visit to the doctor had merely facilitated a hurry up offense so to speak, a two minute drill that had Dan hoping for at least one overtime period. Surely he had worked hard enough for that. I mean, all those salads and fish dinners must account for something.

In the end, after his time had elapsed here, life would go on as usual. It always did. His family and friends would survive just as he had survived past tragedies. If anything else awaited Dan after his time was up he wasn't too concerned. There was nothing he could do about it either way. He didn't need any reward for his time here, just being alive was reward enough. He would have led the same life regardless.

An old Van Morrison song came over his outdoor speakers, as it played Dan watched the top branches on a large Maple tree blow gently in the breeze.

After a time he would return to the computer and work on his crazy novel, but for right now he was going to simply enjoy his moment in the sun. In the distance he heard some young children laughing and screaming, he smiled and allowed all his worries disappear.

"We were born before the wind
Also younger than the sun
Ere the bonnie boat was won as we sailed into the mystic

Hark, now hear the sailors cry
Smell the sea and feel the sky
Let your soul and spirit fly into the mystic

And when that fog horn blows I will be coming home
And when that fog horn blows I want to hear it
I don't have to fear it
I want to rock your gypsy soul
Just like way back in the days of old
Then magnificently we will float into the mystic"
(Van Morrison)

****

Chapter 6

The new sports cars were really sweet thought Danny. The silver
Carrera GT was an awesome machine, it should be for nearly
$450,000. Even with his new windfall Danny would never waste
his money on something that outrageous though. He could pick
up a nice, new Boxter for around 50K and told the salesman to
check around and see what kind of deal he could work out. His
spirits now somewhat lifted, he headed over to meet the lawyer
for perhaps the most important meeting of his entire life. Well,
maybe second most important. The first time he met Liz was tops
on his list. It was in college, psychology 101. Her legs were a real

killer, and she had sort of a bratty kind of attitude as if to say, "forget it buddy, you got no chance."

But in time, their opposite personalities became intermingled and they were soon inseparable. And now, some 35 years later, nothing had changed.

Phil Kersey was a criminal lawyer with 20 plus years of experience. As Danny entered his office he felt a rush of blood go to his head. What was he doing here anyway? How did it come to this?

He met the receptionist and told her who he was.

"Take a seat Mr. Edwards, Mr. Kersey will be with you shortly," she said. The waiting room had two other people in it. Danny glanced briefly at them and wondered what heinous acts they had committed. Of course, they were most likely thinking the same thing about him. Danny considered making small talk with the heavy set gentleman who seemed to be nervously checking his watch and reading a dated magazine.

But he thought better of it, who knows, why get involved in his story.

"So, are you here to see Mr. Kersey too?" Danny blurted out, losing control over his recent decision.

The man looked up from his magazine, "Me, no I'm here to see his partner, Ken."

And he went right back to reading as if to say, leave me alone.

"That went well," muttered Danny under his breath, "I knew I should have just kept my mouth shut."

"I am here to see Phil," the middle aged lady sitting by the window responded. "He is the greatest, let me tell you. If it wasn't for him, I would be back in the Robert Scott Correctional Facility in Michigan, no doubt. And you don't want to spend anymore time in that place than is absolutely necessary. I owe Phil my life, and then some. He never gave up on me." Her voice was scratchy, probably from years of smoking and who knows what else.

The heavy set gentlemen was now getting more agitated. He pursed his lips as if to say, "Enough already, lady." But she went on. "Yeah, Phil and me go way back. I remember the first time I came to him, in deep trouble over some bad checks. Well, the checks were good, there just wasn't enough money in the bank to cover them is all. It wasn't like I was trying to rip anybody off or anything. I mean, shit happens, you know?"

"Yes it does," responded Danny with a certain new found understanding of the term, "Yes it does."

"Mr. Edwards, you can go back now," the professional looking secretary advised him. "The last door on the right."

"Good luck," he offered up as he gladly got out of that weird situation, a nervous fat guy who had nothing to say and a chatty, female ex-con.

Bill Strathmore was making little progress given the information supplied him by Danny. There were so many variables to deal with. It was unlikely he could hack into all the web sites he found on local safe companies and as far as the banks, he could get in serious trouble doing that to them.

He remembered an old army buddy who now worked for the bank in question. Maybe he could do some snooping around. He would call him at home later, who knows, all he can do is refuse. Bill decided to start with the security company who guarded Lakeview Manor. Perhaps he could dig up something on them.

"I can understand why the police want to question you, Mr. Edwards," the attorney responded after hearing Danny's version of the events. "But if that is all there is, then you have nothing to worry about. That is all there is, I assume. Because if there is anything else, anything you are not telling me, then we may have a problem."

"First off, call me Danny. And that is basically what happened, nothing else."

"OK, good, I thought so, but I have to ask. If we go into that police station and they bring up facts I don't have any prior knowledge of, then it can get ugly. And I hate ugly." The lawyer said explaining the seriousness of the situation to his new client. "I'll set up a time for tomorrow morning to meet with them. So right now, let's run through the series of events, step by step. I'll play devils advocate and try to confuse you, make you sound like you are lying, or at least concealing something. That is what the detectives might do, I want you to be prepared for the worst, OK?"

Danny's heart was now pounding and he wished he never went on that late night call.

"She can keep her money and her cat. All I want is my life back," he suddenly retorted. "This is all BS, I didn't ask for any of this."

"Well, ask for it or not, you got it. Calm down and let's go through this. Your first meeting with the detective, on the night in question, let's examine that in detail." The attorney and Danny spent four hours going over testimony.

They took one short break when Mr. Kersey had to deal with his street hardened, female client who apparently had shown up at his office unannounced. When he came back into the office he shook his head.

"My cousin was a plumber, I helped him one summer long ago. Sometimes I wished I had taken up that instead of law. You should see the house he lives in, drives a nice Cadillac too. Bet he doesn't have to put up with nut jobs like that every day either." The lawyer mused to Danny.

"Oh don't worry," Danny shot back, "we get our share of nut jobs too, trust me."

They both laughed and as Danny left the counselors office he felt much better about his situation. He pulled out the brochure from the Porsche dealer and drooled over the selection once again.

"Umm, that's odd," Bill said aloud. He had dug into the security company's background on the net.

"Only in business two years, and they have several good contracts with gated communities already. I wonder how they managed that." Bill explained, now talking to his soon to be wife who had entered the room.

"Probably an illegal pay off and a few kickbacks here and there, wouldn't be the first time dear."

His lovely girlfriend informing him of the obvious.

"True," Bill replied, but why are their kickbacks any better than all the other security companies?"

"Not better, just more of them" she proclaimed.

"Is there that much dough in protecting a bunch of condos?" Bill wondered out loud.

"Apparently there is. Now can we get going? I'm starving and Jessica is hungry too. You said we would all go to the Olive Garden tonight."

"OK, I'm almost done here, just one more second." Bill clicked on a link on the web site.

The link redirected him to the Safeway Safe Company.

He knew there had to be a connection.

The phone rang. It was his old army buddy returning his earlier call.

"Bill, Jeff here. Listen, I know I owe you from boot camp, so here is the scoop. You didn't hear it from me.

Mrs. Horne withdrew $250,000 in cash shortly after she moved into Lakeview Manor. The manager of her branch strongly advised her against it, said it was foolish to keep that kind of money lying around. He even sent an armed assistant with her when she took out the money. Apparently he put it in some newly installed, high tech safe in her basement. That's all I know. Got it?"

"Thanks man, I appreciate it." Bill said as he hung up the phone.

"I guess Smoochy was right." Bill conceded .

"What's that?" she asked.

"You wouldn't believe me if I told you," Bill said. "Lets go eat, I'll explain it all over dinner.

Danny was mentally exhausted when he got home. He went down to the basement to check on the cat. He filled up his food and water dish and sat down on the couch. Smoochy jumped up on his lap and began licking his hand.

"This is all your fault you know. I hope things go well tomorrow at the police station, otherwise you may end up in the kitty shelter down on the north side. Liz has allergies, she can't take care of you.

You will be shit out of luck if the detectives decide to charge me with something. How did I get in this mess in the first place? Damn."

"Quit your whining," Smoochy said. "You will be home by lunch time and you will be a much richer man to boot.

I see that brochure in your back pocket, nice cars. You have excellent taste. I almost got run over by one of those fancy sports cars. Just swerved at the last second. Lucky for them. I would have came back to haunt them for the rest of their miserable lives."

Danny tried to decide if this was real or another dream. He couldn't tell.

"OK wise guy," Danny replied, "tell me more about the safe company and the gate guards?

How do you know about all that? Just where is that safe at anyway?"

Smoochy explained.

" I know because people say things around a cat. They make phone calls and such thinking no one is the wiser. They don't realize a lot of things about us. Our senses are many times greater than theirs.

I watched them put that safe in. I heard the phone calls, I saw the entire plan unfold."

Danny responded, "Well then why didn't you tell your owner about it?"

"It wasn't like that" Smoochy replied, "She just didn't have the ability you seem to have acquired.

Not many humans do. And before we continue, I have to tell you this living in the basement thing is getting old. What am I a third class citizen or something? I know your wife has some issues with animal dander but give me a break here."

"As soon as I get the inheritance, we will move to a larger place, one with a separate living quarters for you, how's that?" Danny offered.

"I suppose that would be alright." the feisty feline replied back.

Danny then asked, "So exactly where is that safe? I really need to know, just in case."
"I would think in your line of work you would have already seen it," Smoochy advised him.

"Danny, I'm home." Liz yelled as she put her briefcase down on the kitchen table.
Danny once again flew off the couch in disbelief. The cat was eating out of his bowl, oblivious to anything other than his gourmet cat food. Danny said, "Hey Smoochy, you there? Can you hear me?"
The white Persian ignored him and continued on with his meal.

Danny and Liz went out to eat, he explained the days events to her over their meal. "I have faith it will work out Dan. Don't worry about it anymore. OK?"
"I suppose I am getting carried away, but can you blame me?" Danny asked.
"No but that stuff about the cat talking to you in your dreams. I mean, that is pretty far out there, even for you Danny." Liz said half joking.
There was a pause of complete silence and then.
"It's by the furnace!!"
Dan yelled in the middle of the crowded restaurant.
"What is?" Liz quizzed back at him.
"The safe, the secret safe. The one hidden that had the 250 grand in it. That's what Smoochy meant when he said in my line of work I should have already seen it. I just know it. The entire thing revolves around that. Now if I can only prove it without sounding crazy."

Danny's cell phone rang. He saw it was Bill but he didn't want to talk on it like many do while they are out at restaurants or movies. He considered that to be rude, so he went into the men's room.

"Hey Bill, what's up?" Danny answered in a somewhat quiet tone.

"Dan, that guard company is paying off someone to get those contracts. They have to be, they have too many of them for such a new firm like that. And there is a link on their web site to the Safeway Safe company. That has to be the contractor who installed that safe for Mrs. Horne. And there's more.

I have it on inside information that she did, in fact, withdraw $250,000 cash, from her bank shortly after she moved into Lakeview. Something is going on. I am heading home, when I get there I'll see what else I can find out."

"I know where the safe is," Danny told Bill.

"Don't tell me, the cat told you," Bill shot back.

"Sort of, I'll explain later, gotta go. Talk to you soon. Thanks, you are the best." And Danny hung up, noticing a man exiting the stall next to him, the same man who heard him yelling in the middle of the dining area, he said. "It's a long story."

The gentlemen simply responded, "Aren't they all?"

"Yes, I suppose they are" said Danny as he left the men's room. He got Liz and they headed home.

A crazy idea occurred to him while driving home. He called Bill back. "Hey Rambo, feel like going on a secret mission tonight?"

"Hell yeah boss, you know it, and I bet I know where to," Bill exclaimed.

"I'll pick you up in 30 minutes, wear something dark." And Danny hung up.

Liz looked at him in amazement. "You're not."

"Oh yes I am," Danny grinned back at her. "I'm going to find that safe."

Danny picked up Bill and saw that he had covered much of his face with some dark make up.

"Getting a little carried away are we?" He asked Bill in a sarcastic tone.

"It's shoe polish, I have some more here, want it?" Bill laughed back.

"Why not, it can't hurt," and Danny smeared some over his face as well.

While driving they came to a red light. For no good reason they looked at each other and broke out laughing hysterically. The tension had gotten to both of them. When the tears quit rolling down their face they noticed a police cruiser pulling out of a side street. Bill slumped down in his seat and Danny put his hand up to the side of his face.

Danny and Bill pulled into the parking lot of the convenience store located a few blocks from Lakeview Manor. It was after 11 p.m. and the store had just closed for the night. Normally a busy location with many residents of the complex coming and going, it was now dark and deserted.

They parked the truck off to the side and crept out making sure no one saw them. From there, they moved down the road and headed through a nearby park to the area that surrounded the condos.

They took turns climbing up over the stucco wall. As Danny hit the ground a dog started furiously barking somewhere in distance. "C'mon Bill, hurry up," Danny nervously whispered.

"I think I got some of that shoe polish crap in my eye, hold on a second," Bill replied.

After wiping his eyes, Bill quickly made his way over the top of the wall. They moved along the back yards staying as far away from the buildings as possible using trees and shrubs for cover. The dog started up again and as Danny looked back he didn't notice the small fish pond that one of the residents had put in. He slipped on a large, wet rock at the pond's edge and went right down on his butt. The barking got louder and they saw a floodlight come on a few houses away. Bill ducked down while Danny sat motionless in the cold water.

"Get in here Rocky, you'll wake the entire neighborhood," a voice rang out. And suddenly the night got quiet. The light went out and Bill grabbed Danny's hand pulling him out of the pond.
"Crap, I think I sprained my ankle," Danny muttered.
Bill was trying not to laugh out loud. "We must be nuts," he finally admitted.
Mrs. Horne's residence was dark, save one light in the living room, which was on a timer, to make it appear someone still occupied the place. The two edged closer, moving with such stealth now that even if someone was gazing out their window they would not be noticed. At the back door Bill took over. He had some small tools and easily opened it. Bill then moved to the security panel located inside to decode it in the necessary time period. He managed to enter a generic code used by service companies when they worked on such systems. Danny had his compact flashlight and headed to the furnace room.
"Now where is it," he quietly remarked. "It has to be here."
"Maybe the cat was lying, ever think of that?" Bill said grinning.
"Maybe he was, or maybe we are both as crazy as a bunch of loons, I'm not sure which," Danny threw back at him. Just at that second Danny noticed something that seemed odd in that furnace area. An old, console television sat next to the return air duct by the furnace. Some books and other junk sat on top of it. Now in most homes this would look quite normal but Mrs. Horne only saved her valuable antiques and other personal effects from days gone by. She used to say she hated a bunch of junk lying around and "when in doubt, throw it out."
She would never keep an old TV lying around, never. Danny moved the books and a few boxes off the top of it. The television wouldn't budge as he tried to wedge it out from the wall. It was anchored down. "Look here Bill," Danny said all excited, "I think I got it."
They both tried to move the television but it wasn't possible. Bill then noticed the back of the set seemed to have a hinge on it. He pulled down hard and it snapped open. There, inside the TV was

the handle of a heavy duty, hardened steel safe with the usual combination cylinder. It was buried in the floor.

"The old bag had it changed on us," A voice coming from the other side of the room caused Danny and Bill to nearly collapse in fear.

As Danny swung his light up on the man he saw the gun, held firmly in his hand, pointing directly at both of them. He recognized the man in the security uniform. It was Harv. The older gentlemen that all the older residents had trusted completely.

"She must have contacted another safe company who changed the combination for her. I guess she wasn't that dumb after all. I couldn't get it open. I didn't mean to kill her, it was an accident, really."

"And I suppose this is also an accident, you standing there pointing that gun at us?" Danny replied back at the gray haired old man who continued on.

"Then you showed up to fix her furnace and I had to get out of here. We were going to come back when things calmed down and crack the safe. But once again, you show up. Now you leave us with no choice."

"You will never get away with this, you must know that," Danny said trying to convince himself as well as the crooked guard, went on. "No way in hell."

" Don't you watch CSI old timer." Bill added.

Danny gave Bill a look as if to say don't make this guy any madder than he already is.

"Yes, I watch it, so?" The guard answering back in a matter of fact tone of voice. "Here is how it unfolds. After a suspicious death in a gated community, an older security guard, already nervous after the recent events, shoots two intruders in an attempted robbery at the same residence. Look at you two clowns. Dark clothes, faces all painted dark, in here in the middle of the night."

"I told you the face paint was a stupid idea," Danny muttered to
Bill.

"Is that why you put it on too?" Bill shot back.

"Enough," the guard cocked his weapon. "I'm tired of this
already, just like I was tired of kissing all the rear ends of those
old rich people. Harv, get me this, do this for me."

"HARV, DROP THE GUN," came a voice from behind him. "Do
it now, or you're dead."

Harv slowly lowered his weapon and let it fall. Detective Wadell
moved out of the shadows and kicked the gun across the room.

"Put your hands on your head, NOW," the detective barked,
sounding like he was in no mood to fool around.

Bill and Danny put their hands on their head.

"Not you two clowns," Wadell said. "I can only guess what you
are up to, not very smart to come back here Mr. Edwards, and as
for your assistant, I'm afraid to ask. You both almost got
yourselves killed you know. What in the hell where you
thinking?" The detective cuffed Harv as back up arrived. "When
surveillance called and said you were snooping around, I got here
pronto. And it is a good thing I did, or else."

"Well officer," Danny explained. "You had scared the bejesus
out of me, what with the formal statement and being a suspect.
I had to prove I was innocent. And finding the safe was the only
way for sure."

"The statement was merely a formality, we were pretty sure you
weren't in on this deal," The detective explained. "We got tipped
off shortly after her death. This isn't the first suspicious crime in
a community guarded by this company. We have been tracking
some things for months. Mrs. Horne's murder was simply the
straw that broke the camels back, so to speak."

"So when you said this was an accident, that first night, when she
died....?" Danny quizzed the policeman.

"We wanted everyone to hear that, if you notice I said it loud
enough so anybody standing nearby, who might be involved,
would let their guard down, including you at that point. In the

days that followed it all became clear. We pieced together the crime ring involving the guard company and some employees at the Safeway safe company. Old Harv here is only a pawn, used by his employers as many others were. There were several robbery's but this appears to be the first murder related to the crime ring."

"It was an accident, I tell you," Harv pronounced.

"We'll let a jury decide that," the detective replied, "Get him out of here." A uniformed policeman whisked Harv into a waiting patrol car.

"Now as for you two," Jim Wadell cautioned. "I don't think I will press any charges. I should but, who would take care of Smoochy if I sent you up the river? So do yourselves a favor, go directly home, wash that stupid shoe polish off your face. I expect to see you both in my office at 10 a.m. for a formal statement concerning this. Mr. Edwards, if you wish to bring along your attorney you may do so but I assure you it will not be necessary. So you can save yourself the $250 an hour he charges if you wish. That's up to you. My guy will ride you back to your truck now, GO."

And the two furnace guys, all dirty, one wet and limping, proceeded out like two puppies with their tales between their legs.

"Hey Danny," the detective added, "Cheer up, you did me a favor. Hearing the confession from Harv was a bonus, it wrapped things up neatly for me. That's another reason I am overlooking your indiscretions here. You did good."

Epilogue

In the months that followed, the crime ring was busted wide
open. Harv was convicted of murder, as any wrongful death
during the commission of a felony is the same as if you pulled the
trigger. His nephew, who was working the gate during the crime,
was convicted as an accessory, as were the owners of the security
company and a couple Safeway Safe Company employees.
Danny finally received his inheritance after agreeing to give each
of Mrs. Hornes two children $200,000.

He could have fought it in probate but her son, Robert who needed the cash due to some poor business dealings, agreed to settle out of court.

And so it was. Danny gave the business to Bill but still offered up his help and advice until Bill got a good grasp on things. It was so enjoyable Danny began a consulting firm for all new business owners. It kept him quite busy and more importantly, a reason to get out of bed in the morning. Liz retired from teaching and took up tutoring to remain active.

They bought a nice place out in the country and often took long weekend excursions to visit their children and of course, their grandkids. They always drove there in the new, silver Porsche. He added on a special barn like room for Smoochy and even got him a companion, a female one. Danny only conversed in his sleep with Smoochy one more time.

It was right after he brought home the female Persian, Darla. During an afternoon nap Danny looked down at Smoochy who was grinning from ear to ear.

Smoochy quietly remarked, "Danny old boy, that new pussycat you brought home, man, she is hot."

****

Dan wrapped up his story. The publishing house agreed to give him a retainer. They wanted a series of books from him, all revolving around his career in the HVAC trades. In time, some Hollywood producers got a hold of them and made a rather successful movie as well.

The telephone rang, it was Dan's doctor.
He turned the music down.

"We were born before the wind
Also younger than the sun
Ere the bonnie boat was won as we sailed into the mystic
Hark, now hear the sailors cry
Smell the sea and feel the sky
Let your soul and spirit fly into the mystic

And when that fog horn blows I will be coming home
And when that fog horn blows I want to hear it
I don't have to fear it
I want to rock your gypsy soul
Just like way back in the days of old
Then magnificently we will float into the mystic"
(Van Morrison)

www.ingramcontent.com/pod-product-compliance
Lightning Source LLC
Chambersburg PA
CBHW052141170626
46812CB00004B/1538